UNDER THE AUTUMN STAR

Books by Knut Hamsun
published by Sun & Moon Press

Victoria
translated by Oliver Stallybrass

The Women at the Pump
translated by Oliver and Gunnvor Stallybrass

Wayfarers
translated by James McFarlane

Rosa
translated by Sverre Lyngstad

Under the Autumn Star
translated by Oliver and Gunnvor Stallybrass

A Wanderer Plays on Muted Strings (forthcoming)
translated by Oliver and Gunnvor Stallybrass

The Last Joy (forthcoming)
translated by Sverre Lyngstad

KNUT HAMSUN

Under the Autumn Star

*

Translated from the Norwegian by
Oliver and Gunnvor Stallybrass

LOS ANGELES
SUN & MOON PRESS
1998

Sun & Moon Press
A Program of The Contemporary Arts Educational Project, Inc.
a nonprofit corporation
6026 Wilshire Boulevard, Los Angeles, California 90036
http//:www.sunmoon.com

First Sun & Moon Press edition published in 1998
10 9 8 7 6 5 4 3 2 1
English translation ©1975 by Farrar, Straus and Giroux, Inc.
Reprinted by permission
Published originally as *Under Høststjærnen*
(Christiana: Gyldendal Norsk Forlag, 1906)
All rights reserved

This book was made possible, in part, through contributions to
The Contemporary Arts Educational Project, Inc.

Cover: Charles Burchfield, *Orion in December,* 1959
National Museum of American Art, Washington, DC
Design: Katie Messborn

LIBRARY OF CONGRESS CATALOGING IN PUBLICATION DATA
Hamsun, Knut [1859–1952]
Under the Autumn Star
p. cm _ (Sun & Moon Classics: 134)
ISBN: 1-55713-343-3
I. Title. II. Series.
811'.54_dc20

Printed in the United States of America on acid-free paper.

Under the Autumn Star

I

*Y*esterday the sea was as smooth as a mirror; it is smooth as a mirror today. The island is having an Indian summer. Such a mild, warm Indian summer! Yet there is no sun.

It is years since I knew such peace, perhaps twenty or thirty years; or perhaps it was in a previous life. Whenever it was, I must surely have tasted before now this peace that I feel as I walk around in ecstasies, humming to myself, caring for every stone and every straw, and sensing that they care for me once more. We are friends.

As I follow the overgrown path through the forest, my heart trembles with an unearthly joy. I remember a spot on the eastern shore of the Caspian where I once stood. The place resembled this one, and then as now the sea was calm and torpid and iron-gray. I walked through the forest, I was moved to tears of rapture, I kept saying, Dear God, to be here again!

As if I had been there before.

But if so I must have gone there, once upon a time, from another age and another land, where the forest and the paths were the same. Perhaps I was a forest flower, perhaps I was a beetle and made my home in an acacia tree.

And now I have come to this place. Perhaps I was a bird and flew these enormous distances. Or a seed in some fruit sent by a Persian trader.

There now: I am clear of the city, with its noise and bustle and newspapers and people; I have fled all that, because the summons came once more from the rural solitude that is native to me. "You'll see, it will all turn out well," I say to myself, and am filled with hope. Ah, but I have fled like this before, and returned again to the city. And fled again.

But this time I am firmly set on finding peace at all costs. For the moment I am lodging here in a cottage, with old Gunhild as my landlady.

The mountain ashes scattered among the conifers have started to shed their berries—heavy clusters of ripe coral-colored berries that fall to the ground with a thud. They harvest themselves and reseed themselves, they squander each year their incredible superabundance; on one single tree I count more than three hundred clusters. And here and there among the hills stand stubborn flowers that refuse to die, although in truth their time is up.

But then old Gunhild's time is up; and does she die? She behaves for all the world as if death was no concern of hers. When the fishermen are messing about on the beach, tarring their traps or painting their boats, old Gunhild goes up to them with lackluster eyes and the shrewdest of business minds.

"How much is mackerel today?" she asks.

"Same as yesterday."

"Then you can keep your mackerel."

And Gunhild makes for home.

But the fishermen know full well that Gunhild is not one to play-act at going: she has been known to walk all the way up to her cottage without one backward glance. And so "Hi there!" they call after her: let's make it seven mackerels to the half dozen today, for an old customer, that is.

And Gunhild buys her fish . . .

Hanging on the lines to dry are red skirts and blue shirts and underclothes of immense thickness; all spun or woven on the island by such old women as are still alive. But hanging out to dry, also, are those delicate sleeveless slips whose wearers are so apt to turn blue with cold, and those mauve woolen vests which resemble twine when stretched. Where do these monstrosities come from? From the city, of course, bought there by daughters in service, by the young girls of today. With careful, infrequent washing they will last for exactly a month. And their owners find themselves deliciously naked as the holes begin to spread.

But there is none of that nonsense about old Gunhild's shoes. At suitable intervals she takes them to a fisherman of similar age and outlook, and has the uppers and soles permeated with a powerful concoction of grease against which water stands no chance. I have seen that stuff being boiled up on the beach: it is made of tallow, tar, and resin.

Yesterday, as I strolled along the beach looking at driftwood and shells and stones, I came upon a fragment of plate glass. How it came there is a mystery to me; to look at it is like looking at an illusion or a lie. It is hard to imagine a fisherman rowing it there, leaving it there, and going away again! I left it where it lay, thick and plain and commonplace—from the window of a streetcar perhaps. Time was when glass was rare, and bottle-green—God bless the olden days when anything was rare!

And now smoke is rising from the fishermen's huts on the southern tip of the island. It is evening; gruel is being prepared. And when they have eaten their supper, decent folk go straight to bed, in order to be up again at dawn. Only the young and foolish continue to slouch around from cottage to cottage, dragging out the time, heedless of their own best interests.

II

A man landed here this morning; he has come to paint the house. But old Gunhild, who is very old indeed, and crippled with arthritis, gets him to start by chopping a few days' supply of wood for the stove. I myself have offered, time and again, to chop that wood; but she thinks my clothes are too good and has steadfastly refused to give me the ax.

The imported painter is a stocky little man with red hair and no beard; I watch him cautiously from a window, to see how he goes about his work. When I see that he is talking to himself, I steal out of the house and listen. If a blow goes astray, he contains himself and says nothing—unless he grazes his knuckles, in which case his irritation vents itself and he says, "Damn! Damnation!"—then looks quickly around and starts humming, to camouflage what he has said.

Why, I know that painter! Only he's no bloody painter—it's Grindhusen, one of my mates from the road-building days at Skreia.

I go up to him, make myself known, chat with him.

It is many, many years since we built roads together, Grindhusen and I: a pair of callow youths who danced along the roads in the sorriest shoes and ate such food as we could scrape up money for. But whenever we had some money to spare, we would throw an all-night Saturday dance in honor of the girls, with our mates as hangers-on, and the woman of the house growing rich on the coffee she sold us. Then we would work with a will for another week, impatient for Saturday to come around again. As for Grindhusen, he was after the girls like a red-haired wolf.

Does he remember the old days at Skreia?

He looks at me, sizing me up, reticent; it takes me a little time getting him to share my memories.

Well, yes, he remembers Skreia.

"And do you remember Anders the File, and Corkscrew? And Petra?"

"Which do you mean?"

"Petra. Wasn't she your sweetheart?"

"Well, yes, I remember her. In fact, I ended up getting hitched to her."

Grindhusen starts chopping again.

"You got hitched to her?"

"Well, yes. That's the way it was. But what was I going to say—ah yes: looks like you've become a big shot, eh?"

"Why do you say that? These clothes? Don't you have a best suit?"

"How much did you pay for that lot?"

"I don't remember, but not a great deal—I couldn't tell you exactly."

Grindhusen looks at me in amazement and bursts out laughing.

"Don't you remember what you pay for your clothes?" Then he turns serious, shakes his head, and says, "No, I suppose you don't. That's how it is when you're well off."

Old Gunhild comes out of the cottage, sees us passing the time of day by the chopping block, and tells Grindhusen to start on the painting.

"So you've turned painter now," I say.

Grindhusen doesn't answer, and I realize that I oughtn't to have said that in front of a third person.

III

For a couple of hours he daubs and smears, and soon the cottage's northern wall, facing the sea, is a gleaming new red.

During the midday break I go out to Grindhusen with a shot of brandy; we lie on the ground, talking and smoking.

"Painter? I'm not *exactly* a painter," he says. "But when someone asks me if I can paint the wall of a house, I figure I can manage that. And if someone asks me if I can do this, that, or the other, I reckon I can manage that too. Hey, that's a mighty fine brandy you've got."

His wife and two children were living six or seven miles away; every Saturday he went home to them. There were also two grown-up daughters, one married; and Grindhusen was already a grandfather. When he had given Gunhild's cottage its two coats of paint, he was to go to the parsonage and dig a well; in the country there was always something that needed doing. And when winter set in and the earth froze solid, he either went logging in the forest or took things easy for a while, until some job or other appeared from nowhere. His family was not too large nowadays, and something would turn up tomorrow as surely as it had today.

"Now if only I had the chance, I'd buy myself some stonemason's tools," says Grindhusen.

"Are you a stonemason too?"

"I'm not *exactly* a stonemason. But when the well's been dug it will have to be lined, that's obvious . . ."

I wander about the island as usual, thinking of this and that. Peace, peace, a heavenly peace speaks to me in muted tones from every tree in the forest. Why, there are hardly any songbirds left, although a number of crows wheel noiselessly from perch to perch. And the rowanberry clusters fall with a thud and bury themselves in the moss.

Maybe Grindhusen is right: maybe it's a universal truth that something will turn up tomorrow as surely as it has today. It's two weeks now since I saw a newspaper, and I'm still alive and well, and making great strides toward inner peace: singing, flexing my muscles, standing bareheaded as I gaze at the stars in the evening sky.

For the last eighteen years I have sat in cafés and complained to the waiter if a fork was not quite clean. Here in Gunhild's cottage I complain about no forks! Did you see Grindhusen, I say to myself: how in lighting his pipe he held the match till the very end and never burned his leathery fingers? I notice, too, that when a fly crawls over his hand he simply lets it crawl; perhaps he never even feels it. That's how a man should be where flies are concerned.

That evening Grindhusen takes the boat and rows away. I roam the beach, singing a snatch or two, throwing stones far out over the sea, hauling driftwood ashore. The stars are out, the moon is up. An hour or two later Grindhusen returns, with a good set of stonemason's tools in the boat. Those are stolen goods, all right, I think to myself. We each shoulder a load and hide the tools in the forest.

By now it is night, and we go our separate ways.

The next afternoon sees the painting of the house completed; but to make up the day Grindhusen agrees to chop firewood until six o'clock. I take Gunhild's boat and go out fishing, in order not to be around when he leaves. I catch no fish; I keep shivering and looking at my watch. Surely he must have gone by now, I say to myself; and around seven o'clock I row home again. Grindhusen has reached the mainland and shouts good-bye to me from there.

A ray of warmth pierces me through and through; it is like a summons from my youth, from Skreia, from a generation back.

I row over to him and say, "Can you dig that well on your own?"

"No, I'll need someone to help me."

"Take me!" I exclaim. "Wait here, I'm just going back to settle up."

I am halfway across before Grindhusen calls out, "No—I need to hurry—night's coming on. Besides, you're not serious, are you?"

"Give me five or ten minutes. I'll be right back."

And Grindhusen sits down on the beach: he remembers that I
have some mighty fine brandy in my hip flask.

IV

It was a Saturday when we came to the parsonage. Grindhusen had finally, and with many misgivings, taken me on as his
assistant. I had bought provisions and working clothes, and
stood now at the appointed place, clad in a smock and top
boots. I was free and unknown; I soon learned to walk with
long, slow steps, and as far as my face and hands were concerned, I already had a proletarian look. We were to live at the
parsonage and cook for ourselves in the washhouse.

And so we started to dig.

I did my full share, and Grindhusen had no complaints.
"You'll make a real good worker yet," he said.

After a while the priest came out to us, and we raised our
caps and bowed. He was a mild, elderly man with a deliberate
manner of speech; the wrinkles that fanned out from his eyes
were like the remnants of a thousand good-natured smiles. He
was sorry to bother us, but his poultry were a perfect nuisance,
straying into the garden year after year; perhaps we could come
and do something about the garden wall first, or rather one particular section of it?

Grindhusen answered, Why, of course, that could certainly
be fixed.

So we went and sorted out the tumbledown wall, and while
we were busy with this, a young lady came out and watched us
for a while. We raised our caps again, and I thought how lovely
she was. Then a teenage boy came out to have a look, and plied
us with questions. I guessed they were brother and sister. The
work went on apace, while the youngsters stood and watched.

Then it was evening. Grindhusen went off home, while I stayed behind, spending the night in the hayloft.

The next day was Sunday. I didn't dare put on my town clothes for fear they should look too smart on the likes of me; but I gave yesterday's outfit a good going over. I spent the mild Sunday morning strolling about the parsonage grounds; I chatted with the farmhands, and joined them in chaffing two of the maids. When the bell began ringing for church, I sent to ask if I could borrow a hymnal, and the priest's son brought me one. From the tallest of the farmhands I borrowed a jacket; it was on the small side, but by taking off my smock and vest, I made it into a passable fit. And so I went to church.

The inner peace that I had been building up during my stay on the island proved quite inadequate as yet: as the organ tones swelled out, I found myself wrenched from my context and ready to burst into sobs. "Shut your trap!" I told myself—"it's only nerves." I had chosen an isolated seat, and I hid my emotion as best I could. I was glad when the service was over.

After dining off the meat that I had cooked for myself, I was invited into the kitchen for a cup of coffee. As I was sitting there, in came the young lady from yesterday. I stood up, bowed, and received a gracious nod in return. How charming she was, with her youth and her dainty hands! When I got up to go, I forgot myself and said, "Thank you so much for your kindness, most gracious lady!"

She looked at me in astonishment, wrinkling her brows and slowly turning crimson. Then she turned and flounced out of the kitchen. She was very young.

Now I'd really messed it up!

Sick at heart, I crawled up into the woods to hide. Impertinent fool that I was, not to have held my tongue! Abysmal old windbag that I was!

The parsonage buildings lay on a little slope, topped by a wooded plateau, with here and there a clearing. It struck me that this plateau was the proper place to dig the well, with a pipe leading down to the buildings. I made an estimate of the height and felt confident that the fall was sufficient. On the way home I paced out the distance, and made it about two hundred and fifty feet.

But what business of mine was the well? Let us not be caught off guard like that again: turning genteel, blurting out affronts, acting above our station.

V

On Monday morning Grindhusen returned and we started to dig. Out came the old priest again: would we mind putting up a post for him on the road up to the church? He needed this post—there used to be one there, till it blew down—needed it for nailing up notices and announcements.

We put up a new post, taking pains to see that it stood as straight as a sentry; then we crowned it with a hood of zinc.

While I was busy on this hood, I got Grindhusen to suggest that the post should be painted red—he still had some red paint left over from Gunhild's cottage. The priest, on the other hand, wanted the post white, and Grindhusen echoed him obsequiously; so I pointed out that white notices would show up better against a red background. Whereupon the myriad wrinkles around the priest's eyes melted into a smile, and he said, "Yes, you're absolutely right."

That smile and those few words of assent were all I needed to make me proud and happy in my inmost being.

The young lady came up and addressed a few words to Grindhusen; she even joked with him, asking him who this red cardinal was that he was installing up here. To me she said nothing, nor did she look my way when I raised my cap.

Dinner was a sore trial. Not that the food was poor; but the way Grindhusen ate his soup, and the glistening pork fat around his mouth, filled me with disgust.

What will he be like eating porridge? I reflected hysterically.

When Grindhusen stretched himself out on the bench for an after-dinner nap, still in the same greasy condition, I let him have it and shouted, "For goodness' sake, wipe your mouth, man!"

He looked at me, then wiped his mouth with his hand.

"Mouth?" he said.

It seemed wisest to laugh it off. "Ha-ha, fooled you there all right, Grindhusen," I said. But I felt dissatisfied with myself and went straight out of the washhouse.

Anyway, I said to myself, I intend Mademoiselle to acknowledge me when I greet her; she'll soon learn that I have my wits about me. That well and water pipe now—what if I came up with a detailed plan! Not having any surveying instruments to determine the fall from the top of the slope, I set to work improvising one. A wooden pipe would serve, with a couple of lamp chimneys let in as uprights, the joints sealed with putty, and the whole thing filled with water.

More and more jobs kept cropping up at the parsonage: a doorstep to be straightened, a foundation wall to be repaired, the hayloft ramp to be put in order before the corn could be brought in. The priest liked having everything in good order, and since we were paid by the day, it was all the same to us. But as the days went by I enjoyed my workmate's company less and less. I was vexed beyond measure by such things as his habit of holding a loaf against his chest and hacking off chunks with a greasy pocket knife that he was constantly licking; not to mention the fact that he never washed from one Sunday to the next. Then there was the glistening dewdrop which, before sunrise and after sunset, invariably hung from his nose. And the state of his nails! And those misshapen ears!

Whereas I, alas, was an upstart with elegant ways picked up in cafés. Unable after a while to refrain any longer from censur-

ing my companion's filthy habits, I caused such bad blood between us that I feared we would sooner or later have to split up.
Meanwhile, we spoke no more than was strictly necessary.

The well remained as undug as ever. Sunday came around
again, and Grindhusen went home.

My surveying gadget was ready by now, and in the afternoon
I went up on the roof of the main building and set it up. I saw
at once that the line of the "sights" cut the slope some fifteen or
twenty feet below its top. Good. Even if I allowed three or four
feet down to the water level in the well, the pressure would be
more than enough.

As I lay there using my "level," I was spotted by the priest's
son—Harold Meltzer was his name. What was I doing up
there? Measuring the slope—what for? Why did I need to
know the height? Please, could he have a look?

Later on I got a thirty-foot line and measured the slope from
foot to summit, Harold helping me. When we came down
again, I presented myself to the priest and outlined my plan.

VI

The priest listened patiently and didn't immediately show me
the door.

"Really?" he said with a smile. "Well, perhaps. But it will
cost a lot of money. And in any case, what's the point?"

"It's seventy yards to the well we've started to dig. Seventy
yards for the maids to walk, no matter what the conditions,
summer and winter."

"Yes, there's that. But it will cost the earth."

"Not counting the well, which you're having in any case, the
actual pipe—material and labor—won't come to more than a
couple of hundred kroner."

The priest sat up.

"Not more?"

"No."

I paused a little over each answer, as if I'd been born with a slow, deliberate nature; but I'd worked it all out a long time ago.

"It would be a great convenience," said the priest thoughtfully. "That tub in the kitchen's certainly a messy business."

"And think of all the water that has to be carried to the bedrooms."

"Ah, the bedrooms would be no better off. They're upstairs."

"We'd run a pipe up there too."

"Can we really do that? All the way upstairs? Will the pressure be sufficient?"

Here I paused even longer over my answer, as if weighed down with the sense of my responsibility.

"I think I can safely promise you a jet that would clear the roof."

"No, really?" exclaimed the priest. "Come, let's see where you propose digging the well."

We went up the slope, the priest, Harold, and I. I let the priest use my gadget and convinced him that the pressure would be more than sufficient.

"I'd better talk to your mate about it," he said.

By way of undermining Grindhusen, I replied, "Why bother? He doesn't understand these things."

The priest looked at me.

"Really?" he said.

We came down again. The priest said, half to himself, "You're right there—it's an endless business fetching water in the winter. In the summer too, for that matter. I'd better discuss it with my family."

And he went indoors.

Ten minutes or so later I was summoned to the front steps, where the whole family was assembled.

"So you're the man who's going to supply us with water pipes?" Madame asked in a friendly tone.

I bowed, slowly and ceremoniously, cap in hand, while the priest answered for me: yes, I was the man.

Mademoiselle looked at me curiously and at once began chatting with Harold. Madame continued to interrogate me: Would it really be the same system they had in the city, you turned on a tap and the water came? And just the same upstairs? A couple of hundred kroner? "Well, I think you should go ahead," she told her husband.

"Ah, you think so? Come on then, let's all go up the hill once again and have a look."

We went up the hill. I set up my "level" and let them look through it.

"Amazing!" said Madame.

Mademoiselle said never a word.

The priest asked, "But is there water here?"

I replied very sagaciously that I couldn't *swear* to it but there were plenty of hopeful signs.

"What signs?" asked Madame.

"The nature of the ground up here. And those willows and alders. Willows need moisture, you know."

The priest nodded and said, "This fellow knows his job all right, Marie."

On the way home Madame reached the fallacious conclusion that she could manage with one maid less if they had running water. To avoid letting her down, I remarked, "Especially in the summer, perhaps. You could water the garden with a hose from the cellar window."

"Fantastic!" she exclaimed.

I didn't venture even to suggest a pipe to the barn. I had realized all along that a well twice the size, with an extension pipe to the barn, would lighten the dairymaid's work as much as it would the kitchen maid's. But this would just about double the cost. To suggest such a grandiose plan was inadvisable.

Even as it was, I had agreed to wait until Grindhusen returned. The priest said he wanted to sleep on it.

VII

I now had the job of breaking it to my mate that the well was to be dug on the plateau; and to avoid arousing his suspicions, I laid all the blame on the priest, making out that it was his idea, which I had merely supported. Grindhusen was quite happy: he saw at once that it would mean more work for us, since we would have to dig a trench for the pipe.

As good luck would have it, on Monday morning the priest began by saying to Grindhusen, half in jest, "Your mate and I have decided to dig the well up on the plateau and run a pipe down—how's that for a crazy idea?"

Grindhusen thought it was a mighty fine idea.

But when we talked it over and went, the three of us, to inspect the site for the well, Grindhusen began to suspect that I'd had more to do with the plan than I was willing to let on. The trench for the pipe, he pointed out, would have to be very deep, because of the frost—

"Four foot six at the most," I interrupted.

—and that would be an expensive affair.

"Your mate figures a couple of hundred kroner in all," answered the priest.

Grindhusen was all at sea where estimates were concerned and could only say, "Yes, well, two hundred kroner is still a tidy sum."

I said, "There'll be less for his reverence to pay in dilapidations when he moves."

The priest started.

"Dilapidations? But I've no intention of moving."

"Then I sincerely hope that your reverence will enjoy the blessings of running water into a ripe old age."

At this the priest stared at me and asked, "What's your name?"

"Knut Pedersen." *

"And where do you come from?"

"From the north."

I knew what these questions were getting at, and resolved never again to talk in that novelettish way.

However, the well and the pipe were decided on, and we set to work . . .

The days that followed were mainly cheerful ones. At first I was very anxious about whether we would find water, and for several nights I slept badly; but once this anxiety was removed, there remained only a plain, straightforward job of work. There was water aplenty: after a day or two we had to bail it out in bucketfuls each morning. The bottom was of clay, and we got in a fine old mess as we squelched around in the well. After a week of digging, we turned to quarrying stones to line the well—a job we both knew inside out from our Skreia days. Then we dug for another week until the well was deep enough. The bottom was now so wet that we had to start lining at once if the clay walls were not to collapse and bury us.

And so we dug and quarried and lined, while week after week went by. It was a big well and a fine job; the priest was quite pleased. Grindhusen and I began to hit it off better again; and when he learned that I wanted no more than a fair laborer's wage, even if on this job it was often I who took command, he was anxious to do something in return, with the result that his table manners became more appetizing. My lot was now perfect: no one was ever going to lure me to the city again!

In the evenings I would wander about the forest, or the churchyard, reading the inscriptions on the tombstones and thinking of this and that. Also, I was looking for a thumbnail,

* Hamsun's real name.—Trans.

from a dead body. I needed this nail for a whim I had, a caprice. I had found a splendid piece of birch root, from which I intended to carve a pipe bowl in the shape of a clenched fist. The thumb was to form a lid, and I wanted to cut a nail into it, to make it really lifelike. The ring finger was to be encircled by a little gold ring.

With such trivialities as these, my mind was soothed and salved. My life was free from hurry, I could daydream without neglecting some duty, the evenings were my own. If possible, I wanted also to work up a little feeling for the sanctity of the church, and terror of the dead. I recalled from long, long ago a profound and luxurious sense of mystery, and it was this that I wished to partake of again. When I found that nail, maybe a cry would arise from the tombs: "That is mine!" Whereupon I would drop the thing in terror and take to my heels.

"How that weathervane creaks!" Grindhusen would say from time to time.

"Are you scared?"

"Not scared exactly—but it gives me the creeps of a night time when I think of all those dead bodies lying so near."

Happy Grindhusen!

One day Harold taught me how to plant fir cones and shrubs. This was a skill I knew nothing about—it wasn't yet taught when I went to school. But once I had learned the technique I became an assiduous Sunday planter. In return I taught young Harold one or two things that were new to him, and we became good friends.

VIII

All might now have been well but for the young lady, of whom I found myself growing daily more fond. Her name was Elischeba, Elizabeth. She was no real beauty, I suppose, but her red lips and blue, girlish glance made her lovely. Elischeba, Elizabeth, you are in the first flush of dawn, and your eyes hold the world in their gaze. When you spoke with young Eric from the neighboring farm one evening, those eyes were all ripeness and sweetness.

It was easy enough for Grindhusen. In his younger days he had been after the girls like a wolf, and he still, from long habit, swaggered around with his hat at a rakish angle. But by now he was well and truly tamed, as was to be expected; such is the course of nature. Still, not everyone follows the course of nature, not everyone is tamed—and what is to become of those others? And now there was little Elizabeth—who, by the way, was far from little, being as tall as her mother. And with her mother's high bosom.

Since that first Sunday I had received no more invitations to coffee in the kitchen; I myself wanted none, shamefaced as I still was, and made it easy for none to be offered. But finally, in mid-week, one of the maids brought me a message: I was not to bury myself in the woods every Sunday afternoon but was to come in for a cup of coffee. Madame had said so.

Good.

Should I dress in my Sunday best? No harm, perhaps, in giving the young lady a hint of who I was: a man who had of his own free will renounced the life of the city and assumed the badge of servitude, but for all that a man with technical flair who knew how to install running water. But by the time I was dressed, I sensed for myself that my workaday clothes suited me better; so I took off my Sunday things and hid them in my bag.

In the event, it was not Mademoiselle who greeted me in the kitchen but Madame. She chatted with me for some time, and she had placed a small white cloth under my coffee cup.

"It looks like that trick with the egg will turn out expensive for us," she said with a good-humored laugh. "The boy's used up half a dozen eggs already."

The trick I had taught Harold was the one of forcing a

shelled boiled egg down through the neck of a decanter by rarefying the air in the latter. It was about the only physics I knew.

"But that experiment with the stick, breaking it in those two loops of paper—that was really instructive," Madame went on. "I don't understand these things, but . . . When will the well be ready?"

"The well *is* ready. Tomorrow we start on the trench."

"How long will that take?"

"About a week. Then the plumber can come."

"Fancy that!"

I thanked her and left. Madame had the habit—retained, no doubt, from earlier years—of giving you an occasional sidelong glance. Yet her words were quite devoid of guile.

And now the leaves on the trees were yellowing one by one, and earth and air were fragrant with autumn. Only the fungus family was out in full display, shooting up everywhere, growing thick and good on chubby stems: cepes, fairy-ring champignons, milk fungus. Here and there a fly agaric flaunted its scarlet cap and flecks of white. That singular fungus! It grows alongside the edible kinds, nourished by the same earth, receiving the sun and rain from heaven on the same terms; it is fat and firm and good to eat—except that it is full of pungent muscarine. I once thought of inventing a magnificent old legend about the fly agaric and saying I had read it in a book.*

I have always enjoyed observing flowers and insects in their struggle for survival. When the sun was hot they would come to life again and abandon themselves for a few hours to their former joy; the big, strong flies were as fully alive as they had been at midsummer. There was a peculiar kind of flea beetle here which I hadn't seen before—little yellow things, no bigger than an 8-point comma, but capable of jumping several thou-

* The Vikings are believed to have been in the habit of eating fly agaric before a battle, with the object of going berserk.—Trans.

sand times their own length. What enormous strength such a creature has in relation to its size! Here comes a little spider with a hindpart like a pale-yellow pearl—a pearl so heavy that the creature can only climb up a blade of grass by turning its back toward the ground. If it meets with an obstacle over which it cannot drag its pearl, it drops down again and starts on another blade. This pearl spider is no mere spider, period. If I hold out a leaf to help it find its feet on a floor, it fumbles around for a little on the leaf before deciding that no, this is not quite right, and drawing back from any such pitfall as a floor . . .

I hear my name being called from the wood below me. It is Harold, my Sunday-school teacher, who has set me a lesson from Pontoppidan's catechism commentary and wants to test me on it. I am moved when I hear religion proclaimed anew, the way I would have liked to proclaim it in my own childhood.

IX

The well was finished, the trench was dug, the plumber had arrived. He chose Grindhusen to help him lay the pipe, while I was put to work in the house, making ready for the pipes leading up from the cellar.

One day, while I was excavating in the cellar, Madame came down. I called out to her to be careful, but she took it very casually. "There's no hole here, is there?" she asked, pointing. "Or here?" Finally she missed her footing and came slithering down into the trench beside me. There we stood. We had no light, and for her, coming in from the daylight, it must have been pitch dark. She groped about the trench and said, "And now can I get up again?"

I lifted her up. It was easy enough: her figure was still very trim for the mother of a big, strong girl.

"Well, I must say!" she exclaimed, shaking the earth from her dress. "That was a good brisk ride . . . I'd like you to help me with something upstairs one of these days, will you? Only we must wait until my husband is over at the chapel—he hates alterations. When do you expect to finish this job?"

I mentioned a period of a week or so.

"And where are you going from here?"

"To the next farm. Grindhusen has arranged for us to harvest potatoes . . . "

Next I came up to the kitchen and sawed a hole in the floor with a compass saw. Miss Elizabeth inevitably had things to do in the kitchen during the time I was busy there, and she overcame her dislike of me enough to say a few words and stand watching the work for a while.

"Imagine, Oline," she said to the maid, "when all you have to do is turn on a faucet."

But Oline, who was old, looked anything but overjoyed. It was blasphemy, she said, making the water come right into the kitchen. For twenty years she had carried in all the water they needed. What was she expected to do now?

"Rest," I said.

"Rest? I thought mankind was made to work."

"And sew things for your trousseau," said Mademoiselle with a little laugh.

It was girlish chatter, but I was grateful to her for taking part in the general conversation and being in the kitchen for a while. And heavens, how intelligent I became, how aptly I talked, how like a boy I plumed myself! I remember it still. But suddenly Miss Elizabeth seemed to decide that it was not proper for her to stay with us any longer and left the room.

That evening I went, as so often before, up to the church-yard; but on seeing that Mademoiselle was there before me, I took myself off and wandered into the forest. Afterward I thought: Now, surely, she will be touched by my modesty and say, "Poor fellow, he showed real delicacy there!" After that it would only remain for her to follow me into the forest. Taken thus by surprise, I would get up from my stone and bow. Then she would be a little embarrassed and say, "I was just passing— it's a lovely evening—what are you doing here?" "Just sitting here," I reply, returning as if from a great distance with my innocent eyes. And when she hears that I am just sitting here late in the evening, then she realizes that I am a deep soul and a dreamer, and falls in love with me . . .

The next evening she was in the churchyard again, and a presumptuous thought came flitting through my head: it was me she was after! But when I looked more closely, I could see that she was doing something to a grave; so it was not me she was after. I crept away to the great ant hill up in the woods and watched the creatures for as long as I could see; then I sat listening to the thud of the spruce cones and rowanberry clusters. I hummed, whispered, pondered; from time to time I had to get up and walk for a bit to keep warm. The hours passed, night came, I was so much in love that I walked bareheaded and let the stars outstare me.

"How late is it?" Grindhusen was liable to ask when I came up to the hayloft.

"Eleven o'clock," I would answer, though it might be two or even three in the morning.

"Is that your idea of bedtime? Ugh, damnation! Waking people up after they've gone right off to sleep!"

Grindhusen would turn onto his other side, and a moment later fall asleep again. It was easy enough for Grindhusen.

But oh, what a fool a middle-aged man becomes when he falls in love. And was it not I who was going to prove by my example that one *can* find peace and quiet?

X

A man turned up to reclaim his stonemason's tools. What—so Grindhusen hadn't stolen them! How boring and mediocre Grindhusen was in all his ways—nothing good and generous about him!

I said, "It's just eat, sleep, and work with you, eh, Grindhusen. There's a man here come for the tools. Why, you only borrowed them, you poor creature."

"You're a fool," said Grindhusen, taking umbrage.

So once again I appeased him by passing off my words as a joke.

"What do we do now?" he asked.

"Come off it—*you* know."

"I know?"

"Sure. If I know you, that is."

And Grindhusen was appeased.

But during the midday break, while I was cutting his hair, I offended him again by suggesting he should give it a good wash.

"It beats me how a man of your age can be so stupid," he said.

And God knows, Grindhusen may have been right. Grandfather or not, he still had his crop of red hair intact . . .

Was the hayloft suddenly haunted? Who had been in there one day and made it nice and tidy? Grindhusen and I each had our own bed space; I had bought myself a couple of blankets, whereas Grindhusen bedded down every night fully clothed, burrowing at random into the hay. And now my pair of blankets had been straightened to give the appearance of a genuine bed. I had no objection: presumably one of the maids wanted to teach me a few folkways. It was all one to me.

And now I was due to go upstairs and saw a hole in the floor, but Madame told me to wait: tomorrow the priest would be over at the chapel, at the other end of the parish, and I wouldn't be disturbing him. In the morning there came a further postponement: Miss Elizabeth was about to go shopping at the store, and I was to go with her and carry all her purchases.

"You go ahead," I said, "I'll follow."

Strange girl! Had she decided to put up with my company? She said, "But will you find the way on your own?"

"Oh yes—I've been there before; it's where we get our food."

Since I could hardly go wandering all over the parish in my clay-stained working clothes, I put on my best trousers, though without changing my smock. Then I set off in pursuit. It was about four miles; over the last mile I kept catching glimpses of Miss Elizabeth ahead of me, but I took care not to follow too hard on her heels. Once she looked around; whereupon I made myself as small as I could and side-stepped into the forest.

Mademoiselle stayed behind at a friend's house, while I returned home with the shopping. I arrived around noon and was invited to eat in the kitchen. The house seemed deserted: Harold was out somewhere, the maids were laundering in the washhouse, only Oline was pottering around in the kitchen.

After dinner I went upstairs and began sawing on the landing.

"Come in here and give me a hand for a moment," said Madame, leading the way.

We went past the priest's study and into the bedroom.

"I want my bed moved," said Madame. "It's too near the stove in winter—it gets terribly hot."

We moved the bed over to the window.

"Don't you think it's better here?" she asked. "Cooler?"

I chanced to look at her: that slanting side glance of hers was fixed on me. Wow! And all at once I was mere flesh and blood and foolishness. I heard her say, "Are you crazy? For goodness' sake—the door—" and then my name whispered again and again . . .

I sawed through that hole on the landing, and finished off the job, while Madame never left my side. She wanted so badly to talk, to explain herself, laughing and crying all the time.

I said, "That picture that was hanging over your bed—hadn't we better move that too?"

"You've got something there," answered Madame.

XI

And now the pipes were all laid, the faucets were turned on, and the water came gushing into the sinks. Grindhusen had found someone else to lend him the necessary tools, so we were able to plaster up a few holes left here and there. Two days later we had filled in the trench leading up to the well and our work at the parsonage was done. The priest was pleased with us, and offered to put up a notice on the red post describing us as expert plumbers; but since by now it was so late in the year that the earth might freeze solid at any moment, this would hardly have helped us. Instead, we asked him to bear us in mind in the spring.

We now moved to the neighboring farm to dig up potatoes. Before leaving we had to promise to look in again at the parsonage whenever we had a chance.

At the new place there was quite an army of workers; we split up into groups and had a fine old time. But the work was unlikely to last for more than a week, after which we would be footloose again.

One evening the priest came over and offered me work on the parsonage farm. The offer was a good one, and I considered it for a while before finally turning it down. I preferred to rove around as a free agent, picking up such work as I could, sleeping out, taking myself a little by surprise. In the potato field I had met a man with whom I wanted to join forces when I parted from Grindhusen. This new man was a kindred spirit and, to judge by what I saw and heard of him, a good worker. Christened Lars Falkberget, he had adopted the name of Falkenberg as better-sounding.

The potato harvesting was done under the direction of young Eric, and it was he who carted the crop away. He was a handsome young man of twenty, mature and reliable for his age, with the self-assurance of the farmer's son. There was evidently something between him and Miss Elizabeth from the parsonage, because one day she came over to the field where we were working and chatted with him for quite a while. Before leaving she found a few words for me too, telling me that Oline had begun getting used to running water.

"And yourself?" I asked.

Out of politeness she said something in reply to this also, but I could see that she had no wish to get drawn into conversation with me.

How prettily she was dressed, with a new light-colored coat to offset her blue eyes . . .

The next day Eric had an accident: his horse bolted, dragged him across several fields, and finally dashed him against a fence. He was badly knocked about and spitting blood. Falkenberg was now promoted to driving the cart.

Though I feigned sympathy over the accident, and was silent and somber with the rest, I felt no grief. I had no prospect of winning Miss Elizabeth, to be sure, but he who had stood above me in her favor was now out of the way.

The next evening I went and sat in the churchyard. If only Miss Elizabeth would come now! A quarter of an hour passed and she came. I rose abruptly, artful to the core, looked as if I wanted to escape, but found myself caught and gave up the attempt. Here my artfulness failed me; I became unsure of myself from having her so near, and I started saying something: "Eric—that was bad luck he had yesterday."

"I know."

"He hurt himself badly."

"Yes, of course he hurt himself badly. Why do you talk to me about him?"

"I thought . . . No, I don't know. But in any case he'll recover, of course. Then everything will be all right again."

"Of course, of course."

Pause.

It sounded as if she had been aping my words. Suddenly she said with a smile, "You're a strange one. Why do you come all this way and sit here of an evening?"

"It's just a way I've got into. To while away the hours until bedtime."

"You aren't afraid then?"

Her joke steadied me, I felt myself on solid ground again and answered, "There's another reason: I wanted to learn to shudder in my shoes again."

"Shudder in your shoes? Like the boy in the fairy tale? Where did you read about that?"

"I don't know. In some book or other, I suppose."

Pause.

"Why don't you want to work on our farm?"

"It wouldn't suit me. I'm joining forces with a new man now. We shall pack our bags and go."

"Where will you go?"

"I don't know. East or west. We're wanderers."

Pause.

"That's too bad," she said. "I mean, you shouldn't do that . . . Now, how did you say Eric was? That's what I came about."

"He's not well, he's in a very bad way, I believe, but . . ."

"Does the doctor think he'll pull through?"

"I imagine so. I haven't heard to the contrary."

"Good night then."

O to be young and rich and famous and a man of learning!
. . . There she goes . . .

Before leaving the churchyard I found a serviceable thumbnail, which I pocketed. I waited a moment or two, peering this
way and that and listening, but all was quiet. No one cried:
"That is mine!"

XII

Falkenberg and I set out on our wanderings. It was evening,
the weather cool, the heavens high as the stars lit up. I per-
suaded my companion to go via the churchyard; absurd creature
that I was, I wanted to see if there was a light in a little window
down at the parsonage. O to be young and rich and . . .

We walked for several hours; our loads were not too heavy,
we were a pair of wanderers still fairly new to each other, we
could talk together. We passed one roadside store and came to a
second; we could see the chapel tower in the clear evening light.

From long habit I wanted to go into the churchyard here
also. I said, "Why don't we bed down in here for the night?"

"A fat lot of sense that makes!" retorted Falkenberg—"when
there's hay in every barn now, and if we're turned out of the
barns, we'll be snugger still in the woods."

And Falkenberg resumed command of our wanderings.

He was a man in his thirties, tall and well-built (though
stooping a little), with a long, drooping mustache. He was on
the taciturn side, but quick-witted and intelligent; moreover,
he had the loveliest singing voice—in short, he was a very different character from Grindhusen. He spoke a crazy mixture of
western and eastern dialects, with some Swedish words thrown
in, so that it was quite impossible to say where he hailed from.

We came to a farm where the dogs barked and people were

still up; Falkenberg asked to speak to the man. A mere lad came out.

Had he any work for us?

No.

But the fence along the road was very rickety—couldn't we do something about it?

No. The man himself had nothing else to do at this time of year.

Could we have shelter for the night?

Sorry, but—

In the barn?

No, the farm girls were still sleeping there.

"The bastard!" muttered Falkenberg as we took ourselves off.

We turned in through a little wood, keeping an eye open for somewhere to sleep.

"Why don't we go back to the farm—to the girls? They wouldn't throw us out, would they?"

Falkenberg thought it over.

"The dogs would bark," he answered.

We came out into a field with two horses in it. One had a bell.

"He's a fine master, he is," said Falkenberg, "leaving his horses in the open and his farm girls to sleep in the barn so late in the year. "Let's do these beasts a kindness and ride them for a bit."

He caught the bell horse, stuffed its bell full of moss and grass, and mounted. My horse was more skittish, and I had more trouble catching it.

We rode across the field, found a gate, and emerged onto the road. We each had one of my blankets to sit on, but neither of us had a bridle.

It went well, uncommonly well: we rode for several miles until we reached another village. Suddenly we heard people on the road ahead of us.

"Time we started galloping," said Falkenberg over his shoulder.

But the long-limbed Falkenberg was not much of a rider: first he grasped the bell strap; then he threw himself forward and clung to the horse's neck. I had a glimpse of one leg silhouetted against the sky as he fell off.

Fortunately we were in no danger: it was only a courting couple.

After another half hour's ride, by which time we were both of us stiff and sore, we slithered to the ground and urged the horses home. Then we continued on foot.

There came a distant "gakgak, gakgak." I recognized the cry of the gray goose. As children we were taught to fold our hands and stand quite still so as not to frighten the gray goose as it flew by; I had nothing to lose by doing the same again now. A serene and mystical mood flickered within me; I held my breath and gazed. There it came, the sky trailing behind it like the wake of a ship. "Gakgak!" came the cry from overhead, as the splendid plow glided onward beneath the stars . . .

Finally we found a barn on a farm where all was silent and slept for several hours—so soundly that the people on the farm surprised us there next morning.

Falkenberg at once addressed the man and offered to pay: we had arrived so late last night, he explained, that we hadn't wanted to wake anyone; but we weren't runaways. The man not only refused payment but even gave us coffee in the kitchen. However, he had no work for us: the harvest was in, and he and his boy had nothing to do themselves except repair the fences.

XIII

We wandered for three days without finding work; instead, we had to pay for our food and drink and were growing steadily poorer.

"How much have you got left and how much have I?" asked Falkenberg. "We'll never get anywhere like this." And he suggested we should try a little stealing.

We talked this over and decided to bide our time. Food was no problem; we could always swipe a chicken or two. What we really needed was ready money, and ready money we meant to have, one way or another—after all, we weren't angels.

"I'm no angel descended from heaven," said Falkenberg. "Here I am, sitting in my Sunday clothes—which are no better than the next man's work clothes. I wash them in the stream and wait for them to dry; if they wear out I mend them; and if I earn a bit extra, I buy some more. That's the long and the short of it."

"Didn't young Eric say you drank like a fish?"

"That young cub! Of course I drink. Food by itself is so boring . . . Come, let's find a farm with a piano."

I thought: A piano on a farm means a certain standard of living—so that's where the stealing begins.

It was afternoon when we came to such a farm. Falkenberg had put on my town clothes in advance, and given me his bag to carry, leaving him free as the wind. Without more ado he went up the front steps and disappeared inside for a while. When he emerged he told me casually that he was going to tune the piano.

Going to *what?*

"Be quiet, you," said Falkenberg. "I've done it before, although I don't go around boasting about it."

And when he fished out a tuning key from his bag, I realized he was in earnest.

I was told to remain within earshot while he tuned.

So I wandered around and whiled away the time; every now and again, when I came to the south side of the house, I would hear Falkenberg in the living room, working at the piano with might and main. He couldn't strike up a real tune, but he had a good ear; and whenever he tightened a string he was careful to loosen it again by exactly the same amount, so that the instrument was no worse than before.

I got into conversation with a youngster working on the farm. He told me he earned two hundred kroner a year—plus board. Up at six-thirty every morning to feed the horses; in the busy season, five-thirty. Work all day, supper at eight. But healthy and content with his peaceful life in this little world. I remember his perfect set of teeth and the beauty of his smile when he talked about his girl. He had given her a silver ring with a gold heart set in it.

"What did she say to that?"

"She was kind of surprised, like."

"And what did you say?"

"What I said? I don't rightly know. Hoped it would bring her luck. She should have had a length for a dress too, but . . ."

"Is she young?"

"Ay. Talks just like a little Jew's harp, she's that young."

"Where does she live?"

"Shan't say. Else it would be all over the parish."

I stood there before him like an Alexander, with the world at my feet, a shade contemptuous of his humble life. When we parted I gave him one of my woolen blankets, which I was finding a burden to carry; he at once declared that his girl should have it—she could do with a warm blanket.

And Alexander said, "If I had to be someone else, I'd choose to be you."

When Falkenberg came out after finishing his work, he was so genteel in his gestures and so stilted in his speech that I could barely understand him. He was accompanied by the daughter of the house. "Now we must transfer our location to the next farm," he said, "where there may well be another piano requiring inspection. Adieu, mademoiselle, adieu!"

"Six kroner, boy!" he whispered in my ear. "And six at the next farm makes twelve."

And off we went, with me carrying the bags.

XIV

Falkenberg's hunch was correct: the next farm was not going to be outdone—the piano must be tuned. The daughter of the house was away from home, but the work could be done in her absence as a little surprise. She was always complaining about the untuned piano and how impossible it was to play. At this stage I was again left to my own devices, while Falkenberg occupied the living room. When it grew dark he procured a light and continued tuning. He even had his supper there; after which he came out and demanded his pipe.

"What pipe?"

"You fool—the clenched fist!"

Somewhat reluctantly I handed over my ingenious pipe, which I had just completed, with the nail and the gold ring and a long stem.

"Don't let the nail get too hot," I whispered, "or it may curl up."

Falkenberg lit the pipe and went swaggering in with it. But he took good care of me too, asking on my behalf for food and coffee in the kitchen.

I found myself a place to sleep in the barn.

During the night I was woken by Falkenberg standing in the middle of the barn and calling my name. The moon was full and the night clear; I could see my companion's face.

"What is it?"

"Here's that pipe of yours."

"Pipe?"

"Yes, I'm damned if I'll keep it any longer. Look at it—the nail's working loose."

I took the pipe and saw that the nail had curled up.

Falkenberg said, "It was just as if it was making faces at me in the moonlight. And then I remembered where that nail came from . . ."

Happy Falkenberg!

Next morning we were on the point of leaving, when the daughter of the house came home. We heard her hammering out a waltz on the piano; then she came out and said, "Yes, there's a world of difference. Thank you *so* much."

"Mademoiselle is satisfied?" asked the maestro.

"Yes, indeed: there's quite a different tone to it now."

"And where does Mademoiselle recommend that I go next?"

"To Øvrebø, to the Falkenbergs."

"To the *who?*"

"The Falkenbergs. You follow the road straight on and after a couple of miles or so there's a signpost on the right. That's where you turn off."

Whereupon Falkenberg sat down abruptly on the steps and proceeded to cross-examine Mademoiselle about the Falkenbergs of Øvrebø. Fancy meeting his relatives here—it was almost like coming home! His particular thanks to Mademoiselle: it was a most signal service that she had rendered him.

And off we went again, with me carrying the bags.

Once in the wood we sat down for a council of war. Was it advisable for a Falkenberg with the rank of piano tuner to turn up on the Captain's doorstep at Øvrebø and be his kinsman? I was the timid one, and my doubts infected Falkenberg. All the same, it might be rather amusing.

Had he no papers with his name on them? Testimonials?

"Yes, but bloody hell, all they say is that I'm a capable workman."

We wondered whether to tamper with the references a little; but it seemed better to compose one from scratch. Then it could refer to a piano tuner of genius and be made out in the name, not of Lars, but of Leopold. We had a free hand.

"Can you undertake to write that reference?" he asked.

"Certainly I can."

But now my poor stiff imagination spoiled everything by running away with me. A piano tuner was a cipher; I would make him a mechanical genius, credit him with solving the most complicated problems, give him a factory—

"A factory owner doesn't need references," Falkenberg interrupted, and refused to listen to me any more. No, the whole thing seemed to be fizzling out.

Gloomy and dejected, we continued on our way until we reached the signpost.

"So you're not going?" I said.

"You can go," answered Falkenberg angrily. "Here, take your rags and tatters."

But when we were some way past the signpost, Falkenberg slackened his pace and muttered, "All the same, I can't bear to see it thrown away. A chance like that."

"In that case I think you should pay them a call. After all, it's by no means impossible that you really are related to them."

"I wish I'd thought of asking if he has a nephew in America."

"Would you have talked English in that case?"

"Oh, do shut your trap and keep it shut. I don't know what you've got to be so pleased with yourself about."

Overwrought and out of temper, Falkenberg strode on again. But almost at once he stopped abruptly and said, "I'll do it. Lend me your pipe again. I won't light it."

We walked up the hill. Falkenberg put on a great act, pointing now and then with the pipe and airing his views about the way the manor was situated. Somewhat irritated by the arrogant way he strutted along, while I carried the bags, I said, "So you're a piano tuner again?"

"I think I've proved I can tune a piano," he answered curtly. "And that's that."

"But supposing the lady knows a bit about it? And tries the piano afterward?"

Falkenberg fell silent; I saw him chewing it over. With every step his bearing became less erect, his stoop more pronounced.

"Perhaps it's unwise," he said. "Here, take your pipe. We'll just go up and simply ask for work."

XV

As it happened, we were able to make ourselves useful the moment we arrived at the manor. A new flagpole was being raised, and they were short of hands; we joined in, and raised the pole in triumph. There were women watching from every window.

Was the Captain at home?

No.

Madame?

Madame came out. She was tall and fair, and as friendly as a young foal—how prettily she acknowledged our greeting!

Did she by any chance have work for us?

"I don't know. No, I don't think so. You see, my husband's away."

I got the impression that she found it hard to say no, and I began replacing my cap so as not to worry her. But Falkenberg must have struck her as exotic, with his correct dress and his private porter; she looked curiously at him and asked, "What kind of work?"

"Any kind of outdoor work," answered Falkenberg; "we can do fencing, ditching, masonry—"

"Isn't it a bit late in the year for that kind of work?" put in one of the men by the flagpole.

"Yes, I suppose it is," Madame agreed. "I don't know—but it's dinnertime now; perhaps you'd like to go in and have a bite of food? Whatever we're having."

"I don't mind if I do," said Falkenberg.

I was much put out by this vulgar answer, which did us no credit at all. It was time I got a word in.

"*Mille grâces, madame, vous êtes trop aimable,*" I said gallantly, at the same time taking off my cap.

She turned and looked at me for a moment. Her surprise was comical to see.

We were shown into the kitchen and given an excellent meal.

Madame too went indoors. We had finished eating and were about to leave when Madame came out again. Falkenberg had regained his courage and was eager to take advantage of her friendliness. He asked if he might tune her piano.

"Do you tune pianos too?" she asked, wide-eyed.

"Indeed I do. I've tuned several around here."

"Mine's a grand, and naturally I wouldn't want . . ."

"Madame can rest assured."

"Do you have any . . ."

"I've no references. I'm not in the habit of asking for them. But Madame can hear for herself."

"Well, all right—come this way."

She led the way and he followed. As they went in, I had a glimpse of a room with many pictures on the walls.

The maids were bustling to and fro in the kitchen, eyeing me, the stranger; one of them was very pretty. I sat and thanked my stars that I had shaved that morning.

Ten minutes or so went by; Falkenberg had begun his tuning. Madame came back into the kitchen and said; "Well, well, so you speak French. That's more than I do."

Thank goodness, that was the end of the matter. On my side it would have been almost entirely a matter of letting them eat cake, and looking for the woman, and the state being me.

"Your friend has shown me his testimonials," said Madame. "You seem capable fellows, both of you. I don't know—I could telegraph my husband and find out if we have any work for you."

I wanted to thank her, but couldn't get a word out; I started to swallow.

Nerves.

So I took a little tour of the manor and the surrounding fields. Everything was in good order, the harvest under cover—even the rackloads of potato stalks, which in many places are left in the open until the first snow. I could see nothing for us to do. The people here were evidently rich.

As it drew on toward evening and Falkenberg was still tuning the piano, I took some of my provisions and wandered off, to avoid being invited to supper. The moon and the stars were out, but I chose to grope my way into the densest part of the forest and sit there in the dark. Besides, it was more sheltered there. How peaceful the earth was, and the air too! It was growing chilly, with frost on the ground. From time to time came a faint crackling in the straw, the squeak of a mouse, the flapping of a crow above the treetops—then complete silence again. Have you ever in all your life seen such fair hair? No indeed. Born glorious from top to toe, mouth ripe and lovely beyond words, shimmer of dragonflies in her hair. O to have a diadem to take from one's bag and present to her! I shall go and find a pale-pink shell and carve a nail from it, then I shall give her the pipe as a present for her husband, yes, that is what I shall do . . .

Back at the manor Falkenberg met me outside and hurriedly whispered, "She's heard from her husband: we can fell timber in the forest. Have you ever done any felling?"

"Yes."

"Go into the kitchen, then. She's been asking for you."

I went in, and Madame said, "Where did you get to? Please come and eat. You *have* eaten? Where?"

"We have food in our bags."

"You shouldn't have done that. Won't you have a cup of tea then? Are you sure? . . . I've heard from my husband. Can you fell trees? Ah, that's splendid. Look: TWO LOGGERS NEEDED, PETER WILL SHOW MARKED TREES . . ."

Dear God—she stood beside me, pointing at the telegram, her breath fragrant with young woman.

XVI

In the forest. Peter, who had shown us the way there, was one of the farmhands.

When we talked about it, Falkenberg was by no means overwhelmed with gratitude to Madame for finding us work. "There's no cause to go down on our knees," he said; "workmen are scarce around here." Falkenberg, by the way, was no better than average as a logger, whereas I had gained experience in another part of the world and could, if necessary, take command for the present. And indeed Falkenberg himself agreed that I should do so.

And now I began to busy myself with an invention.

With the ordinary felling saws in use today, you have to lie awkwardly on the ground and pull *sideways*. That is why so little work gets done in a day and why the forests are so full of mutilated stumps. By using a conical transmission system attached firmly to the tree's root, it should be possible to saw in the ordinary back-and-forward way, but with the blade cutting horizontally. I began sketching the various parts of such a machine. What gave me the biggest headache was the gentle pressure that the blade of the saw would need. It might be obtained by a compression spring wound up like a clock, or perhaps by a weight. A weight would be simpler, but would remain constant, and as the saw bit more deeply, it would drag more and more and cancel out this pressure. A steel spring, on the other hand, would unwind as the cut grew deeper and would always give the right amount of pressure. I decided on the spring. You wait and see, I said to myself. You can do it. And it would be the proudest moment of my life.

The days went by, one day much like another: we felled nine-inch timber, we lopped and topped. Our fare was rich and good: we took packed lunches and coffee with us into the forest, and had a hot meal when we came home in the evening. Then we washed and tidied ourselves up, in order to be a cut above the farmhands, and sat with the three maids in the kitchen, where a large lamp was burning. Falkenberg and Emma became sweethearts.

And every so often a wave of melodious sounds would reach us from the grand piano in the living room; every so often, also, Madame would look in on us, exuding young-womanhood and blessed friendliness. "How did it go in the forest today?" she would ask. "Did you see the bear?" But one evening she thanked Falkenberg for the good job he had done on the piano. What—really? Falkenberg's weatherbeaten face became handsome with pleasure, and I felt positively proud of him when he answered modestly, "Yes, I was thinking myself it's a little better."

Either his piano tuning had improved with practice or Madame was thankful that he hadn't made her piano any worse.

Every evening Falkenberg dressed himself up in my town clothes. It would never have done for me to claim them back and start wearing them myself; the other would simply have believed that I'd borrowed them from my mate.

"You keep the clothes and I'll have Emma," I said as a joke.

"All right, take Emma" was Falkenberg's reply.

It dawned on me that a coolness had sprung up between Falkenberg and his girl. Poor Falkenberg had followed my example and fallen in love. What a pair of utter boys we were!

Up in the forest, Falkenberg would ask, "Think she'll look in on us again this evening?"

And I might answer, "I don't mind how long the Captain stays away."

"Nor me. Listen, if I hear he's treating her badly, watch out for sparks."

Then one evening Falkenberg chanced to sing a song; and once again I was proud on his behalf. Madame came out, he was asked to repeat that song and then to sing another; his fine voice filled the kitchen, and Madame said, in awestruck tones, "But—I've never heard anything like it!"

That was when I began feeling envious.

"Have you had lessons?" asked Madame. "Do you read music?"

"Yes," answered Falkenberg, "I belonged to a society."

But here, I thought, he should have said no, he had never been lucky enough to have lessons.

"Have you ever sung to an audience? Has anyone heard you?"

"I've sung at dances occasionally. And once at a wedding."

"But has anyone who knows something about music heard you?"

"I couldn't really say. Well, yes, I suppose so."

"Do sing something more!"

Falkenberg sang.

I thought: It will end up with him being invited into the living room one evening, with Madame at the piano. I said, "Excuse me, but isn't the Captain due home soon?"

"Ye-es." Madame's answer was like a question. "Why do you ask?"

"I was thinking about the work."

"Have you felled all the marked trees already?"

"No, not yet, only . . . No, far from it, only . . ."

"Well?" said Madame; then she had an idea. "I don't know—but if it's money . . ."

I clutched at that straw and said; "Well, I would be grateful."

Falkenberg said nothing.

"Dear me, you mustn't be afraid to speak up. Here!" she said, and handed me the money I had asked for. "And you?"

"Nothing, thank you," said Falkenberg.

Dear God, another defeat, another plunge to earth! While the infamous Falkenberg sat there playing the rich man who needed no advance! Before the night was out, I would tear the clothes from off his back, strip him naked!

Which, of course, I never did.

XVII

And the days went by.

"If she looks in this evening," Falkenberg would say up in

the forest, "I'll sing the song about the poppy. I'd forgotten about that one."

"Haven't you forgotten about Emma too?" I asked.

"Emma? Shall I tell you something? You're just the same as ever."

"Am I?"

"Through and through. You'd gladly take Emma in full view of Madame; I couldn't do that."

"You liar!" I answered indignantly. "You won't find *me* chasing after a bit of skirt as long as I'm here."

"No, and from now on I won't be doing any night duties either. Do you think she'll look in this evening? I'd forgotten about the poppy until now. Listen."

Falkenberg sang about the poppy.

"You're a lucky devil with your singing," I said; "but don't imagine that either of us is going to get her."

"Get her, indeed! You really are a prize monkey!"

"Ah, if I was young and rich and handsome, I'd get her all right," I said.

"Ah yes, *if*. In that case I'd get her too. But then what about the Captain?"

"Yes, and what about you? And what about me? And what about herself and the entire world? And what about the pair of us shutting our big, ugly mouths where she's concerned?" I said, furious with myself for my part in this childish chatter. "What sort of rubbish is this for two elderly loggers to be talking?"

We both grew thin and pale, and Falkenberg's suffering face was lined and furrowed; we had lost our former appetite for food. To conceal our respective conditions from each other, I went around whistling cheerful tunes, while Falkenberg boasted at every meal about how he was overeating and getting stiff and ungainly in consequence.

"Why, you're not eating anything," Madame would say when we brought home uneaten the greater part of our packed lunch. "You're a fine pair of loggers."

"It's Falkenberg," I said.

"Huh, it's *him,*" said Falkenberg; "he's given up eating entirely."

From time to time, when Madame asked us to do her a favor, some small service or other, we would both rush to perform it; finally we took to bringing water to the kitchen unasked, and fetching in firewood. Once Falkenberg cheated me out of bringing home from the forest a bunch of hazel twigs to beat carpets with, which Madame had expressly asked me and no one else to cut for her.

And still he continued to sing in the evenings.

This was when I hit on my plan for making Madame jealous. Come, come, my good man, are you mad or merely stupid? Madame won't give your scheme as much as a thought!

All the same, I wanted to make her jealous.

Of the three maids, only Emma was worth considering for my experiment; so I began flirting with Emma.

"Emma, I know of someone who's sighing for you."

"Where did you learn that from?"

"From the stars."

"I'd much sooner you'd learned it from someone here on earth."

"I have too. At firsthand."

"He's talking about himself," said Falkenberg, nervous about being dragged in.

"Very well then, I'm talking about myself. *Paratum cor meum.*"

But Emma was disagreeable and showed no inclination to talk to me, for all my ability to outshine Falkenberg at languages. What—couldn't I even get the upper hand over Emma? After that I became extremely silent and proud, and went my own ways, and made more drawings for my machine, and small-scale models. And in the evenings, when Falkenberg sang and Madame listened, I took myself off to the servants' hall and stayed there with the farmhands—a much more dignified line. The only drawback was that Peter was ill in bed and could not endure the noise of an ax or a hammer; so I had to go to the outhouse every time I needed to strike a good hard blow.

But from time to time I fancied that, in spite of everything, perhaps Madame regretted my being lost to the kitchen. It certainly looked that way. One evening while we were having our meal she said to me, "I hear from the men that you're working on a machine."

"It's a new kind of saw he's fooling around with," said Falkenberg; "but it's going to be too heavy."

I let that pass; I was cunning and chose to suffer in silence. Was not lack of recognition the fate of every inventor? Wait a little, my moment had not yet come. At times I could scarce contain the urge to reveal my identity to the girls, how I was really a gentleman's son whom love had led astray and who now sought consolation in the bottle. Ah yes, very true, man proposes, God disposes . . . And in time it might even reach Madame's ears.

"I've a good mind to start joining you in the servants' hall of an evening," said Falkenberg.

And I knew very well why Falkenberg had suddenly taken a fancy to the servants' hall; for whatever reason, he was no longer invited to sing as often as before.

XVIII

The Captain was back.

A big, full-bearded man came up to us in the forest one day and said, "I'm Captain Falkenberg. How's it going, boys?"

We greeted him respectfully, thanked him, and said it was going all right.

We talked for a bit about the trees we had felled and the trees that remained; and the Captain praised us for leaving such short, neat stumps. Then he calculated how much we had done per day and said it was about average.

"The Captain is forgetting to allow for Sundays," I said.

"You're right," he replied. "In that case it's above average. Any damage? Saw all right?"

"Yes."

"No injuries?"

"No."

Pause.

"You shouldn't really be getting your board from me," he said; "but if you prefer it that way, we can sort it out when we settle up."

"We'll accept what the Captain decides."

"That's right," added Falkenberg.

The Captain took a quick turn through the forest and came back.

"You couldn't have better weather," he said. "No snow to clear away."

"No snow, that's true. But we could do with a bit more frost."

"What for? Are you too hot?"

"Well, yes, that too. But mainly because the saw goes more easily in frozen wood."

"You're an old hand at this work?"

"Yes."

"Is it you who sings?"

"No such luck. He's the one."

"Ah, so *you're* the singer? We're namesakes, eh?"

"Well, yes, in a way," answered Falkenberg, a shade embarrassed. "I'm Lars Falkenberg, as my testimonials show."

"Where are you from?"

"Trøndelag."

The Captain returned home. He was friendly but brisk and decided: never a smile, never a joke. His face was good, if unremarkable.

48

From now on Falkenberg sang only in the servants' hall or in the open air; the Captain's arrival put an end to the singing in the kitchen. Falkenberg chafed over this and spoke dark words to the effect that life was hell and that one might just as well choose a day and hang oneself. But his despair was short-lived. One Sunday he went back to the two farms where he had tuned pianos and asked for testimonials. On his return he showed me the documents and said, "They'll do to keep body and soul together at a pinch."

"So you're not going to hang yourself?"

"You've more cause for that than I have," answered Falkenberg.

But I too was feeling less despondent. As soon as the Captain heard about my machine, he wanted to know more. He saw at a glance that my drawings were inadequate, having been made on absurdly small bits of paper and without even a pair of compasses; he lent me a handsome set of drawing instruments and taught me a bit about constructional calculation. He, too, was afraid my saw would prove too cumbersome. "But carry on," he added; "get it all drawn up on a fixed scale, then we shall see."

However, I knew that a reasonably accurate model would give a better idea of the thing, and when I had completed the drawings, I set about making a model in wood. Having no lathe, I had to cut the two cylinders and the various wheels and screws by hand. I was so absorbed in this that I failed to hear the bell for Sunday dinner. The Captain came and shouted, "Dinner!" Then he saw what I was up to, and offered to drive over to the blacksmith the very next day and get everything I needed turned on a lathe. "Just give me the measurements," he said. "Don't you need some tools as well? A backsaw. Good. Drills. Screws. A small chisel. Anything else?"

He noted it all down. You couldn't have had a better man to work for.

But that evening, when I had eaten and was on my way to

the servants' hall, I heard Madame calling to me. She was standing in the courtyard, in the shadow between the kitchen windows; but now she stepped forward.

"My husband noticed that—well, that you're rather thinly clad," she said. "I don't know if—here, take these!"

And she thrust a complete suit into my arms.

I mumbled and stammered some thanks: I would soon be able to afford a suit for myself, there was no hurry, I didn't need any—

"Oh, I know you can afford it, of course, but your friend has such good clothes, and you—oh, go on, take them."

She fled indoors, exactly like a young girl who's afraid of being caught showing too much kindness. I was obliged to call after her with my final thanks.

The next evening, when the Captain came with my cylinders and wheels, I seized the opportunity of thanking him for the clothes.

"Oh—er—yes," he answered. "It was my wife who thought . . . Do they fit you?"

"Oh yes, they fit."

"That's good. Yes, it was my wife who . . . Well, here are the wheels. And the tools. Good night."

Evidently they were both equally given to good deeds. And when they had done one, each blamed the other. This must be, here on earth, the marriage that dreamers have dreamed of.

XIX

And now the forest is bare of leaves and bereft of bird song; only the crows rasp out their cries at five in the morning, as they spread out over the fields. We see them, Falkenberg and I, as we make our way to the forest; the fledgling birds, which have not yet learned to fear the world, hop at our feet in the path.

We meet the finch, that sparrow of the woods. He has already made a tour of the forest, and now he is on his way back to the humans he likes being with and getting to know from every angle. The strange little finch! He is a bird of passage, really; but his parents have taught him that one *can* survive a winter in the north; and now he in turn will teach his children that one can *only* survive it there. But he still has the migrant blood in his veins, he is still a wanderer. So one day he gathers with his flock and journeys the length of many a parish, to a quite different set of human beings whom likewise he means to get to know—and suddenly the aspen groves are empty of finches. And a whole long week may pass before another flock of these flying creatures settles once more in the aspen groves . . . Dear God, the times I have watched the finch, the entertainment he has given me!

Falkenberg tells me one day that he is right side up with the world again. This winter he intends, by felling timber and tuning pianos, to put aside a hundred kroner, and to make it up with Emma. I too, he adds, should stop sighing after ladies of high degree and go back to my equals.

He is right.

On Saturday evening we knocked off rather earlier than usual, in order to make some purchases. We needed shirts, tobacco, and wine.

Standing in the village store, I caught sight of a little shell-studded sewing box, such as sailors used to buy in Amsterdam in the old days, and bring home for their sweethearts; now the Germans make them in thousands. I bought the box, meaning to make the thumbnail for my pipe from one of the shells. "What do you want with that sewing box?" asked Falkenberg. "Is it for Emma?" His jealousy was aroused, and not to be outdone, he bought Emma a silk handkerchief.

On the way home we started drinking the wine and became talkative. Falkenberg was still jealous. So I selected the shell I needed, broke it off, and gave him the box. After that we were friends again.

It began to grow dark and there was no moon. Suddenly we heard accordion music from a house up on the hill. We figured there must be a dance going on—the light came and went like a lighthouse beam. "Come on, up we go," said Falkenberg.

We were in high spirits.

Outside the house we came upon a group of boys and girls standing in the cool night air; Emma was among them.

"Why, there's Emma!" cried Falkenberg cheerfully; he was not at all put out by her having gone there without him. "Emma, come here, I've got something for you."

He thought a civil word was all she needed; but Emma turned on her heel and went indoors. When Falkenberg tried to follow, he found his way blocked, and it was made clear to him that he had no business there.

"But Emma's there, don't you see? Tell her to come out."

"She's not coming out. She's with Mark, the shoemaker."

Falkenberg was beaten. He had gone around for so long showing his indifference to Emma that she had given him up. While he lingered there as if struck by a thunderbolt, some of the girls began making fun of him: had the poor little kitten lost his mitten, and did he begin to cry?

In full view of everyone Falkenberg put his bottle to his lips and drank; then he wiped it dry with his hand and passed it to his neighbor. Feelings toward us improved: we were good sorts, we had bottles in our pockets, we were ready to pass them around; besides, we were newcomers to the place, we added a touch of variety. And Falkenberg cracked all manner of jokes about Mark, the shoemaker, whom he insisted on calling Luke.

The dance was still going on indoors, but none of the girls chose to desert us for it. "I bet Emma's wishing she was out here with us now," said Falkenberg boastfully. Instead, there was Helene and Rønnaug and Sara, each of whom shook hands in the pretty, traditional way after a swig from the bottle; while others, more sophisticated, merely said, "Your very good health." Helene became Falkenberg's girl: he put his arm around her waist and claimed her for his night duty. When they edged farther and farther away from the rest of us, no one called them to heel; one after another, we paired off and went our ways into the forest. I had acquired Sara.

When we emerged from the forest again, Rønnaug still stood there, in the cool night air. What a strange girl—had she remained standing there throughout? I took her hand and chatted to her a little; she merely giggled at everything I said and made no answer. When we began moving toward the forest, we heard Sara calling after us in the darkness, "Come, Rønnaug, we'd better be going home now!" But Rønnaug made no answer; a girl of few words. She was large and placid, with skin the color of milk.

XX

The first snow had fallen; it melted immediately, but winter could not be far away. And our work in the forest for the Captain was drawing to an end; we had perhaps two weeks left. What should we turn our hands to then? There was work to be had on the mountain railway, or we might pick up more logging somewhere else. Falkenberg favored the railway.

But my machine would not yet be ready. We each had our problems. In addition to the machine, I needed to complete that thumbnail for the pipe, and the evenings were going to be too short for me; while Falkenberg had to make it up with Emma—a slow and difficult business. She had been seeing Mark, the shoemaker, granted; but then Falkenberg had, in an emotional moment, evened the score by presenting the girl

Helene with a shell-studded sewing box and a silk handkerchief.

Falkenberg was in a fix. He said, "Whichever way you turn, it's nothing but trials and tribulations and stupidity."

"Really?"

"That's my view, if you really want to know. She won't be coming with me to the mountains."

"Is it Mark, the shoemaker, who's keeping her back?"

Falkenberg glowered in silence.

"I never went on with my singing either," he said by and by.

We started talking about the Captain and Madame. Falkenberg had a nasty feeling that things were not right between them.

The gossipmonger! I said, "Excuse my saying so, but you don't know the first thing about it."

"Is that so?" he answered angrily. And getting more and more heated, he said, "Have you ever seen them following each other around, or billing and cooing to each other? I've never once heard them exchange two words together."

The idiot! The loud-mouthed idiot!

"What's the matter with your sawing today?" I jeered. "Just look at that cut you've made!"

"*I*'ve made? There are two of us, aren't there?"

"Ah well, perhaps the wood's thawed out too much. Let's try the ax again."

For a long time we chopped away on our own, speaking only in angry monosyllables. What was that lie he had had the impudence to utter—that they never said a word to each other? But, by God, he was right! Falkenberg had a nose for such things, he understood people.

"Well, at least they speak nicely about each other to us," I said.

Falkenberg continued chopping.

I considered it further.

"Well, you may be partly right, it may not be the marriage that dreamers have dreamed of; still . . ."

This was wasted on Falkenberg; he had no idea what I was

talking about. During the midday break I resumed the conversation. "Didn't you say that if he treated her badly I was to watch out for sparks?"

"I did indeed."

"And have there been any sparks?"

"Have I ever said he treats her badly?" asked Falkenberg indignantly. "No, they're bored with each other, that's what. When one comes in, the other goes out. If he starts saying anything in the kitchen, her eyes glaze over and she doesn't take in a word."

We did another long spell of chopping, each of us immersed in his own thoughts.

"I may have no option but to beat him up," said Falkenberg.

"Who?"

"Luke . . ."

I completed the pipe and sent it to the Captain via Emma. The thumbnail looked completely natural, and the excellent tools I had acquired enabled me to inlay it in the thumb and fasten it from below without the two tiny copper nails being visible. I was pleased with my work.

While we were eating our evening meal, the Captain came out into the kitchen to thank me for it. Falkenberg's shrewdness was instantly confirmed: no sooner had the Captain entered the room than his wife left it.

The Captain congratulated me on the pipe and asked how I had fastened the thumbnail; he said I was an artist, a real master. The entire kitchen stood listening to this; and when the Captain called someone a master, his words carried some weight. I believe that at that moment I could have had Emma.

That night I succeeded in learning how to shudder.

A female corpse visited me up in the loft and held out her left hand to show me: the thumbnail was missing. I shook my head: I had had a nail once upon a time, but I had thrown it away and used a shell instead. But the corpse continued to stand there, and I continued to lie there, ice-cold with terror. Finally I managed to say that I was sorry, but there was nothing more that I could do about it; she had best be on her way, in God's name. And our Father, which art in Heaven . . . The corpse came right up to me; I thrust out my two clenched fists, gave a chilling scream—and found myself crushing Falkenberg flat against the wall.

"What is it?" Falkenberg yelled. "For the love of Christ!"

I woke up, bathed in sweat, opened my eyes, and lay watching the corpse slowly fade into the darkness of the room.

"It's the corpse," I groaned. "She wants her nail back." Falkenberg sat up in bed with a jerk; he too was wide awake.

"I saw her!" he said.

"You too? Did you see her thumb? Ugh!"

"I wouldn't be in your shoes for anything."

"Let me go next to the wall!" I implored him.

"Where am I to go, then?"

"You're not in any danger, you can safely go on the outside."

"So she can come and get me first? No, thank you."

And with that Falkenberg lay down again and pulled the blanket over his eyes.

I toyed with the idea of going down and sleeping with Peter; he was on the mend by now and couldn't infect me with his illness. But I was afraid to face going down the steps.

I had a dreadful night.

In the morning I searched high and low for the nail, and found it on the floor among the sawdust and shavings. I buried it on the way to the forest.

"The question is whether you don't have to return the nail to where you took it from," said Falkenberg.

"But that's miles away, a full-scale journey . . ."

"You may be required to make it, all the same. She may not want to have a thumb in one place and a thumbnail in another."

But I felt so well again, the daylight had given me so much bravado, that I laughed at Falkenberg for being so superstitious and told him his outlook had been rendered obsolete by science.

XXI

One evening a carriage drew up at the manor, and since Peter was still unwell and the other farmhand only a boy, it fell to me to look after the horses. A lady got out of the carriage. "The Captain and his wife are at home, I believe?" she said. The clatter of wheels brought faces to the windows, lamps were lit in rooms and on landings, Madame came to the door and called, "Is that you, Elizabeth? I've been waiting and waiting for you. Welcome!"

It was Miss Elizabeth from the parsonage.

"Is *he* here?" she asked in surprise.

"Who?"

It was me she meant. She had recognized me . . .

Next day the two young ladies came out to us in the forest. At first I was afraid that word might have reached the parsonage about a certain ride on borrowed horses, but when I heard no mention of the subject I relaxed.

"The water pipe is working well," said Miss Elizabeth.

That was good to hear.

"Water pipe?" asked Madame.

"He's fixed up a water pipe for us. Into the kitchen and up the stairs. We just turn on a tap. You ought to have one too."

"I see. Could it be done here?"

I answered, yes, it could certainly be done.

"Why haven't you told my husband?"

"I mentioned it to him. He wanted to discuss it with Madame."

An embarrassing silence. He had never even mentioned to her a topic which concerned her as closely as this.

To break the silence I blurted out, "In any case, it's too late in the year now. Winter would be on us before we could finish the job. But maybe in the spring."

Madame returned as if from a great distance.

"Come to think of it, I do remember him mentioning it once," she said. "And our talking it over and deciding it was too late in the year . . . Elizabeth, isn't it fun watching trees come down like this?"

We sometimes used a rope to guide the tree when it fell, and Falkenberg had just fastened this rope high up on a tree, which was already swaying.

"Why do you do that?"

"To guide the tree in the right direction . . ." I started to explain.

But Madame cut me short, repeating her question point-blank to Falkenberg, and adding, "Aren't all directions the same?"

So Falkenberg was obliged to step in.

"Oh no, we have to guide it. To prevent it from crushing too many saplings as it comes down."

"Did you hear," Madame asked her friend, "did you hear that voice of his? He's the one who sings."

I could have bitten my tongue off for talking so much and not sensing her wishes! Well, I would show her that her reprimand was not lost on me. Besides, it was Miss Elizabeth and no one else that I loved; she wasn't temperamental, and she was every bit as pretty as the other, yes, a thousand times prettier. I would sign on at her father's place . . . Meanwhile, I made it a rule, whenever Madame addressed me, to look first at Falkenberg and then at her, and to hesitate over my answer as if nervous of speaking out of turn. I think this behavior of mine was beginning to worry her; and once she said with a timid smile, "Goodness me, it was you I asked."

That smile and those words . . . My heart raced for joy, I began chopping with all the strength and skill I had acquired, I made some splendid cuts; the work seemed more like play. I caught only occasional snatches of what was being said.

"I'm to sing for them this evening," said Falkenberg when we were alone.

Evening came.

I stood in the courtyard and exchanged a few words with the Captain. We had about three or four days' work left in the forest.

"Where do you go next?"

"To work on the railway."

"Perhaps I can make use of you here," said the Captain. "I'm going to rebuild the drive down to the main road—it's too steep as it is. Come with me and I'll show you."

He led me to the south side of the house and began pointing, although it was already quite dark.

"And by the time the road's finished, and one or two other things, it should be spring," he said. "And then there'll be the water pipe. Not to mention Peter being ill; we can't go on like this, I must have more help."

Suddenly we heard Falkenberg singing. The living room was lit up, and Falkenberg was in there, being accompanied on the grand piano. A wealth of melodious sounds floated out to us from that remarkable voice; against my will, I found myself trembling.

The Captain started and looked up at the windows.

"Still"—he said suddenly—"maybe the road too had best wait till the spring. How many days' work did you say you had left in the forest?"

"About three or four."

"Right, let's say those three or four days and then finish for this year."

That was a remarkably quick decision, thought I to myself. Aloud I said, "There's nothing against making a road in the winter; in some ways it's better then. There's blasting to be done, crushed stone to be laid in—"

"Yes, I know, but . . . No, I'd better go in and listen to the singing."

The Captain went indoors.

I thought: He did that from politeness, of course; he wanted to help do the honors when Falkenberg had been invited into the living room. But if the truth were known, he was happier chatting with me.

How conceited I was, and how mistaken!

XXII

The main parts of my saw were now completed and I could assemble them for testing. Near the ramp to the hayloft stood the stump of a wind-felled aspen. I fastened my gadget to this stump and straightway satisfied myself that the saw could cut. Now then, hearken ye, my people, the problem is solved! For a saw blade I had bought myself an outsize backsaw and equipped it with teeth along the full extent of its back; when you sawed, these teeth engaged a small cogwheel which was driven forward by the compression spring. The spring itself I had originally made from a broad corset busk that Emma had given me, but this had proved in earlier experiments to be too slack; and so I had made myself a new spring from a saw blade only six milli-meters across, having first removed its teeth. This time the spring proved too powerful: I had to manage as best I could by winding it only halfway and repeating this process each time it unwound.

My trouble was lack of theoretical knowledge: I had, nearly all the time, to proceed by trial and error, and this made the work very slow. For example, the conical transmission system had proved too cumbersome, and I had had to abandon it en-tirely in favor of a simpler system.

It was a Sunday when I fastened my machine to the aspen stump; the fresh white woodwork and gleaming saw blade spar-kled in the sun. Soon there were faces at the windows, and the Captain came out. He never answered my greeting; he was too intent on the saw as he approached.

"How's it going?"

I started to saw.

"Why, I do believe . . ."

Madame and Miss Elizabeth came out, all the maids came out, Falkenberg came out. And I kept the saw going. Now then, just hearken ye, all my people!

The Captain said, "Won't it take too long fastening the thing to every single tree?"

"Some of the time lost will be made up by the work being much easier. This way you'll never need to stop for a breather."

"Why not?"

"Because the *lateral pressure* comes from the spring. That's the pressure that tires you out most."

"And the rest of the lost time?"

"I intend to discard this screw-on arrangement and to use instead a clamp operated by a sharp depression of the foot. The clamp will have a series of notches and will fit any size tree."

I showed him my drawing of this clamp, which I hadn't had time to complete.

The Captain now had a go at the saw, to see for himself how much strength it needed. He said, "I wonder whether it won't be too heavy, pulling a saw twice the width of an ordinary felling saw?"

"Well, of course," said Falkenberg. "That's obvious."

Everybody looked first at Falkenberg and then at me. Now it was my turn.

"One man can push a fully loaded goods wagon along a railroad track," I answered. "Here you'll have two men to push and pull a saw that slides over two rollers, which in turn run on two steel wires lubricated with oil. This saw will be considerably easier to handle than the old kind; at a pinch it could be worked by one man."

"I figure that's hardly possible."

"We shall see."

Miss Elizabeth asked, half in jest, "But can you explain to an ignorant person like me what's wrong with sawing a tree straight across in the old-fashioned way?"

"He wants to eliminate the lateral pressure for the men sawing," explained the Captain. "With this saw you can actually make a horizontal cut with the same kind of pressure you need for a saw that cuts vertically downward. Look: you press down and produce a sideways cut." He turned to me. "Tell me, don't you think there's a danger of depressing the blade at the ends and making a convex cut?"

"In the first place, the two rollers that the saw rests on will prevent that."

"Yes, they should help. And in the second place?"

"In the second place, you couldn't make a convex cut with this saw if you tried. Because the blade has a T-shaped back which makes it virtually impossible to bend."

I fancied that some of the Captain's objections were made against his own better judgment: with his knowledge, he himself could have answered them better than I. However, there were other points, not raised by the Captain, which worried me. A machine which was going to be carted around in the forest must not have too delicate a mechanism. For example, I was afraid of the two steel wires taking a knock and either breaking altogether or getting bent so that the rollers would jam. I would have to do without the wires and set the rollers under the back of the saw. My machine was still far from ready . . .

The Captain went up to Falkenberg and said, "I imagine you've no objection to taking the ladies on a long drive tomorrow? Peter's not well enough yet."

"Lord, no, I've no objection."

"It's to take the young lady back to the parsonage," the Captain explained as he turned to go. "You'll need to be on the road by six o'clock."

Falkenberg was delighted at this mark of confidence, and

amused himself by accusing me of envy. I was not, in point of fact, the least bit envious. For a moment, perhaps, I was slightly hurt at my mate being preferred to myself, but beyond question I would sooner be on my own in the quiet of the forest than sit shivering on a coachman's box.

Falkenberg, who was in high spirits, said, "You're turning so green with envy, you'd better take some castor oil for it."

He spent the whole morning messing around with preparations for the journey: washing the carriage, oiling the wheels, checking the harness. And I helped him.

"I don't believe you're capable of driving a coach and pair," I said to tease him. "Never mind, I'll teach you the essentials before you set out tomorrow."

"It's too bad you're in such a state, and all for the want of a little castor oil," he retorted.

We continued in this merry, joking vein.

In the evening the Captain came to me and said, "I wanted to spare you and send your mate with the ladies, but Miss Elizabeth insists on having you."

"Me?"

"Because she knows you already."

"But she'd be quite safe with my mate too."

"Do you object to going?"

"No."

"Good. You go, then."

My immediate thought was: Aha, so it's me the ladies prefer after all, because I'm an inventor and a saw owner, and quite good-looking when I'm all spruced up—fantastically good-looking, in fact.

But to Falkenberg the Captain had given an explanation which shattered my vanity at a blow: Miss Elizabeth was to bring me back to the parsonage so that her father could have another shot at engaging me as a farmhand. It had all been arranged between her father and herself.

I pondered and pondered over this explanation.

"But if you sign on at the parsonage, that puts an end to our working on the railway," said Falkenberg.

I answered, "I'm not signing on."

XXIII

Early next morning I set out with the two ladies in the closed carriage. At first it was bitterly cold, and I made good use of my woolen blanket, draping it alternately around my knees and over my shoulders as a shawl.

I followed the road along which I had wandered here with Falkenberg and recognized one landmark after another: here a piano that Falkenberg had tuned, there another; that was where we had heard the gray goose . . . The sun rose, it grew warm, the hours passed. At a crossroads the ladies knocked on the carriage window, saying it was time for lunch.

I could tell from the sun that it was much too early for the ladies' lunch, although well enough on for mine, accustomed as I was to eating with Falkenberg at noon. So I drove on.

"Aren't you going to stop?" the ladies shouted.

"You're used to eating at three, you know . . . and I thought . . ."

"But we're hungry."

I drove to the side of the road, unharnessed the horses, gave them their fodder, and fetched them water. Had these strange people adjusted their mealtime to mine?

"Luncheon is served!" one of them called.

Feeling I couldn't very well join the others for this meal, I remained standing by the horses.

"Well?" said Madame.

"If you'd be kind enough to give me a bite," I said.

The pair of them plied me with food and feared I wasn't get-

ting enough; and when I had opened the bottles, I got my full
share of beer, too; it was a regular roadside banquet, a small
fairy tale in my life. Madame I hardly dared to look at, lest she
should have occasion to feel hurt.

They talked and joked together, and showed their friendliness
by drawing me into it all. Miss Elizabeth said, "Oh, I *do* think
it's fun eating out of doors. Don't you?"

"It's nothing new for him, of course," said Madame. "He has
a meal in the forest every day."

Ah, that voice, those eyes, that tender womanly expression in
the hand holding out the glass toward me . . . And now I,
too, might have said something for myself, entertained them
with a tale or two from the great wide world, or set them right
when they chattered away and showed their ignorance of how
one rides a camel or harvests grapes . . .

I hastened to finish my meal and retire again. I took the
buckets and went, quite unnecessarily, to fetch more water for
the horses; then I sat down beside the stream.

After an interval Madame called for my services.

"You must come back to the carriage. We're going to see if
we can find some wild hops or something."

But as I reached the carriage they were agreeing that the hop
season was over and that there were no rowanberries around
here, or gaily colored leaves.

"There's nothing to be found in the woods," said Mademoiselle. Then she asked me another direct question: "Tell me,
you've no churchyard here to wander about in, have you?"

"No."

"How do you manage without?" And she explained to Madame what a strange fellow I was, wandering around the
churchyard at night in company with the dead, and how that
was where I invented my machines.

For the sake of saying something, I asked her about young
Eric. Hadn't his horse bolted, hadn't he been spitting
blood . . . ?

"He's on the mend," answered Mademoiselle sharply. "Shouldn't we be on our way again, Louise?"

"Yes, can't we be off?"

"Whenever you wish," I replied.

And we drove on again.

The hours passed, the sun sank, the air turned chilly again, and raw; later on we had wind and wet—half rain, half snow. We passed the chapel, a roadside store or two, and farm after farm.

A tap on the carriage window.

"Wasn't it here you went riding on borrowed horses one night?" Mademoiselle asked with a laugh. "We heard all about that, you know."

The two ladies had a good laugh over it.

I hit on a retort.

"And yet your father still wants to take me on as one of his hands, I believe."

"Yes."

"While we're on the subject, miss, how did your father know I was working for Captain Falkenberg? When you yourself were surprised to see me there?"

She thought quickly, then answered, with a glance at Madame, "I wrote and told them."

Madame lowered her eyes.

I had the impression that the girl was lying; but her admirable answer silenced me. There was nothing improbable about her saying to her parents, in one of those letters full of rural gossip, something like: "And guess who I've met here? The man who laid our water pipe, he's here cutting timber for the Captain . . ."

But when we arrived at the parsonage the new hand had already been engaged—had been working there, in fact, for the last three weeks. It was he who took charge of our horses.

So I pondered and pondered once again: why had I been chosen as coachman? Perhaps it was meant as a small consolation for Falkenberg's being invited to sing in the living room. If so, did these people not realize who I was—a man on the point of perfecting an invention, a man who had gone beyond the need for charity?

I was short and sharp with everyone, and weary of myself. I ate in the kitchen, received Oline's blessing for the running water, and went to look after my horses. At twilight I retired to the hayloft with my blanket . . .

I was awakened by fumbling hands.

"But you mustn't sleep here, you know, you'll freeze to death," said the priest's wife. "Come, I'll show you."

We discussed it for a little. I had no desire to move and got her to sit down instead. A creature of fire she was, a daughter of nature. And her inmost being re-echoed still to the strains of a ravishing waltz.

XXIV

Next morning I was in a better frame of mind: calm again, and reasonable, and resigned. If only I had known what was best for me and never left this place; I could have been taken on here and put in charge of all the other hands. Yes, and dug myself nicely into a peaceful rural life.

Mrs. Falkenberg was standing in the yard: a human column, light in color, standing free in the spacious courtyard, without a hat.

I bade her good morning.

"Good morning!" she called back, and advanced slowly toward me. Then she said, very quietly, "I wanted to see where they put you last night, but I couldn't get away. Or rather, I got away, but . . . you didn't sleep in the hayloft, did you?"

I heard the last words as if in a dream and couldn't answer.

"Why don't you answer?"

"You mean, whether I slept in the hayloft? Yes, I did."

"Did you really? Was it all right?"

"Yes."

"I see. Yes, of course. We're going home later today."

She turned and went, her face one crimson glow.

Harold came and asked me to make him a kite.

"Very well, I'll make you a kite," I answered in my confusion, "an enormous kite that will sail right up into the clouds. I promise you that."

We worked for a couple of hours, Harold and I, he so kind and innocent in his eagerness, I for my part thinking of anything but the kite. We gave it a tail several yards long; we pasted and knotted and lashed. Twice Miss Elizabeth came and watched. She may have been as sweet and lively as ever, but I was indifferent to what she was and never gave her a thought.

I was told to harness the horses—an order which I should have obeyed at once, for the way home was a long one; instead, I sent Harold in to ask for another half hour, and we went on working until the kite was ready. Tomorrow, when the paste was dry, Harold could fly his kite, following it with his eyes and feeling an unfamiliar excitement, as I did now.

The horses were harnessed.

Madame appeared at the door; the priest and his family too. Both the priest and his wife knew me again, returned my greeting, and said a few words; but I heard nothing about my signing on as one of their hands. And the wife's blue eyes were fixed on me in that slanting side glance of hers as she knew me again, although she had also known me the night before.

Miss Elizabeth brought food for the journey and wrapped her friend up well.

"Are you sure you've got enough over you?" she asked for the last time.

"Thank you, I've more than enough. Goodbye, goodbye."

"Now, see you drive as nicely as you did yesterday," said Mademoiselle, and nodded to me also.

We drove off.

The weather was cold and raw, and I realized at once that Madame was none too well protected by the blanket she had.

We drove for hour after hour; the horses knew they were homeward bound and trotted unasked. I had no mittens, so my hands grew stiff around the reins. As we passed a cottage set back a little from the road, Madame knocked on the window to announce it was time for lunch. When she got out she was pale from the cold.

"We'll have our lunch up in that cottage," she said. "Follow me when you're ready, and bring the basket with you."

And with that she wandered off up the slope.

It must have been the cold that made her want to eat in a stranger's cottage, I thought; surely she wasn't afraid of me . . . I tethered the horses, fed them, and, since it looked like rain or snow, fastened their oilskins over them. Then I patted them and took the basket up to the cottage.

An old woman living in the cottage welcomed me in, and continued making coffee. Madame unpacked the basket and said, without looking at me, "I suppose you'd like me to fill your plate again today?"

"That would be most kind."

We ate in silence. I sat on a little bench near the door, with my plate beside me; Madame sat at the table, looking out of the window for the most part and eating scarcely a thing. From time to time she would exchange a few words with the old woman, or glance at my plate to make sure it wasn't empty. The little room was so cramped that I was no more than two paces from the window; which meant that we sat together, willy-nilly.

When the coffee arrived, there was no room for my cup on the bench, so I sat holding it in my hand. Then Madame, slowly turning her face toward me, said with downcast eyes, "There's room here, you know."

I heard my heart beat violently and muttered something in reply. "Thank you, I'm fine . . . I'd just as soon . . ."

Beyond doubt, she was uneasy, afraid of my saying some-thing, doing something; once more she sat with her face aver-ted, but I saw how her breast was heaving. "Relax!" I wanted to say; not a word would escape my wretched lips.

I needed to put the empty plate and cup back on the table but feared my approach would frighten her, since she continued to sit with her face averted. I rattled my cup a little to catch her attention, then brought her my things and thanked her.

She tried to put on her hostess voice. "Won't you have some more? Why, you've hardly . . ."

"No, thank you very much . . . Shall I start packing up? If I can, that is."

I had chanced to look at my hands: in the warmth of the cot-tage they had swollen up hideously, and were now so shapeless and clumsy that I was scarcely capable of packing up. She fol-lowed my train of thought, looked first at my hands and then at the floor, and said with a smile, "Have you no mittens?"

"No, I don't need them."

I went back to my seat and waited for her to pack up, so that I could carry the basket. Suddenly she turned her face toward me again and asked, still without looking up, "Where do you come from?"

"From the north."

Pause.

I ventured to ask in turn, "Has Madame been there?"

"Yes, as a child."

As she said this, she glanced at her watch as if to preclude further questions, and also to remind me of the time.

I rose at once and went out to the horses.

It was already growing dark; the sky was overcast and sleet had started to fall. I quietly pulled my blanket down from the box and hid it under the front seat inside. That done, I watered and harnessed the horses. Shortly afterward Madame came walk-ing down the slope; I walked toward her, intending to go for the basket.

"Where are you going?"

"For the basket."

"You needn't bother, thank you. It's not worth taking."

We came to the carriage; she got in, and I made as if to help her wrap herself up. Thus I found the blanket under the front seat; I kept the border well out of sight, to prevent her from recognizing it.

"Well, this is a stroke of luck!" she exclaimed. "Where did you find it?"

"Here."

"I could have got more blankets at the parsonage, but the poor people would never have got them back . . . Thank you, I can manage for myself . . . No, thank you, I can manage . . . Get ready to start."

I closed the carriage door and mounted the box.

If she knocks on the window again, I thought, it will be about the blanket this time; and I'm not stopping.

Hour after hour went by, it grew pitch-dark, the rain and snow fell with increasing violence, the going became worse and worse. Once or twice I jumped down from the box and ran alongside the horses to get warm; the moisture poured off my clothes.

We were nearing home.

I thought: As long as there aren't too many lights blazing, so that she recognizes the blanket . . .

The whole place was lit up, worse luck; Madame was expected.

In desperation I pulled up the horses some way short of the entrance and opened the carriage door.

"What's the matter?"

"I wondered if you'd be kind enough to get out here. The going is so bad . . . the wheels . . ."

She must have thought I was trying to lure her out into heaven knows what. She said, "For goodness' sake, drive on!"

The horses moved on and drew up exactly where the lights were most dazzling. Emma came out to receive her mistress—

who handed her the blankets, having folded them in readiness while she sat in the carriage.

"Thank you for driving!" she said to me. "Heavens above, how wet you are!"

XXV

A surprising piece of news awaited me: Falkenberg had signed on as one of the Captain's hands.

This nullified our agreement and left me on a limb. I couldn't understand it at all. Ah well, time to think about that in the morning. By now it was two o'clock, and still I lay awake, shivering and brooding. All these hours I had been unable to get warm; now suddenly I found myself too hot and lay there with a high fever . . . How frightened she had been yesterday: hadn't dared to eat with me by the roadside, had never once looked me in the face . . .

In a lucid moment it occurred to me that I might wake Falkenberg with my restless turning, and perhaps talk deliriously. Clenching my teeth, I leaped out of bed, pulled on my clothes again, tumbled downstairs, and bounded away over the fields. After a while my clothes began to warm me, and I headed for our forest work place, with sweat and rain streaming down my face. If only I could find the saw and work the fever out of my limbs—my tried and tested cure from of old. I couldn't find the saw, but I found the ax where I had hidden it on Saturday evening and started to chop. It was so dark I could hardly see a thing; but I kept feeling the cut with my hand and felled several trees. I was drenched in sweat.

When I felt sufficiently exhausted, I hid the ax in the same place and ran home at the first glimmering of day.

"Where have you been?" asked Falkenberg.

I didn't want him to know about my catching cold yesterday,

and maybe gossip about it in the kitchen, so I mumbled something to the effect that I hardly knew where I'd been.

"I suppose you've been with Rønnaug," he said.

I said yes, I'd been with Rønnaug, since he'd guessed already.

"It was hardly a guessing matter," he said. "As for me, I don't go out visiting any more."

"You've got Emma now, I suppose?"

"Looks like it. It's a shame you can't stay on here too. Then you might have had one of the others."

Falkenberg enlarged on this theme, how I might have had my pick of the other girls, only the Captain had no more need for my services. I wasn't even to go to the forest today . . . His words came to me from far away, across an approaching ocean of sleep.

By the time morning had fully arrived, my fever had gone; I was a little faint, but began all the same preparing to work in the forest.

"You don't need to wear your woodcutting outfit any more," said Falkenberg. "I've told you once already."

Why, so he had! Nevertheless, I put my forest clothes on, simply because the others were so wet. Falkenberg was a little shy with me because he had broken up our partnership; his excuse was that he had thought I was going to sign on at the parsonage.

"So you're not coming with me to the mountains after all?" I asked.

"Hm. No, I suppose not. But surely you understand. I'm tired of bumming around. And I couldn't find a better place than this."

I pretended it made little difference to me, I took a sudden interest in Peter: it was worst for him, poor man, being thrown out and made homeless.

"Homeless indeed!" retorted Falkenberg. "He'll stay here for the full quota of weeks he's allowed to be sick by law, and then he'll go home. His father's got a farm of his own."

Then Falkenberg declared that our splitting up made him feel as if he were only half a man. If it wasn't for Emma, he would sell the Captain down the river.

"Here," he said, "you can have these."

"What are they?"

"They're the references. I won't need them now, and they may help you out of a tight spot—if you ever feel like tuning a piano."

And he handed me not only the documents but the tuning key as well.

But without Falkenberg's keen ear, I had no use for these items, and I told him I could as easily tune a grindstone as a piano.

At which he exploded with laughter and felt better, because I continued clowning to the end . . .

Falkenberg had gone. Since I could afford to be idle now, I lay down fully dressed on the bed, resting a little more and reflecting. Ah well, we had finished our work, we would have had to leave in any case, I could hardly expect to stay here forever. The only factor outside all our reckoning was Falkenberg's remaining behind. If only I had been the one taken on, I would have worked hard enough for two! Couldn't I buy Falkenberg off? Come to think of it, I had even seemed to detect in the Captain distaste at this workman going around the place with *his* name. But perhaps I had been mistaken.

I brooded and brooded. To the best of my knowledge I had, after all, been a good worker, and I had never stolen one second of the Captain's time in order to work on my invention . . .

I fell asleep again and was awakened by footsteps on the stairs. Before I could get myself properly out of bed, the Captain stood at the door.

"That's all right, don't get up," he said pleasantly and started to leave. "Still, now that I've woken you, perhaps we could settle up?"

"Thank you. As the Captain wishes."

"I ought to tell you that your mate and I both thought you were going to sign on at the parsonage, and so . . . And now the good weather's over, there's no more felling to be done—not that there was in any case. What was I going to say? I've settled up with your mate, I don't know if . . ."

"I'm content to accept the same, naturally."

"Your mate and I agreed you should have slightly more per day."

Falkenberg had mentioned no such thing to me; it must be the Captain's idea.

"I agreed with him to share and share alike," I said.

"Ah, but you were the foreman. Naturally you should have an extra fifty øre per day."

Seeing my disclaimer had not been appreciated, I let him work it out as he pleased and took the money. I remarked that it was more than I had expected.

"Glad to hear it," said the Captain. "And I'd like to give you this testimonial for work well done."

He handed me the paper.

He was a straightforward, upright man. If he said nothing about installing a water pipe in the spring, he doubtless had his reasons, and I shrank from bothering him.

"So you're going to work on the railway?" he asked.

"I don't honestly know."

"Ah well, it's been nice having you here."

He went to the door.

Wretch that I am, I could contain myself no longer. I asked, "Mightn't the Captain have some work for me later on, in the spring?"

"I don't know, we'll have to see. I . . . It all depends. If you find yourself in these parts, then . . . What do you intend doing with your machine?"

"If I may be so bold as to ask if it can stay here—"

"Of course."

When the Captain had gone, I sat down on the bed. Well, that was that; yes, and God be with us all! . . . Nine o'clock—she is up; there she is, walking about in the building that I can see from my window. Let me clear out and have done with it.

I got out my sack and packed it, put the wet jacket on over my smock, and was ready to go. But then I sat down again.

Emma came and said, "Breakfast is ready—come and eat!"

To my horror she had my blanket over her arm.

"And Madame said I was to ask if this blanket is yours."

"Mine? No—I've got mine here in this sack."

Emma went out with the blanket.

How could I possibly admit it was mine? Devil take the blanket! . . . Perhaps I should go down and have something to eat. Then I could say goodbye and thank you at the same time. That would not be too conspicuous.

Emma returned with the blanket and placed it, neatly folded, on a stool.

"If you don't come now, your coffee will be cold," she said.

"Why are you putting that blanket there?"

"Madame said I was to do so."

"Well, I suppose it could be Falkenberg's," I muttered.

"Are you leaving now?" Emma asked.

"Yes, since you won't have anything to do with me."

"Oh, you're impossible!" she exclaimed, with a toss of her head.

I followed Emma down into the kitchen; as I sat at the table, I saw the Captain on his way to the forest. I was glad to see him gone; now, perhaps, Madame would show her face.

I finished my meal and got up. Should I go now without more ado? Of course. So I said goodbye to the girls, with a few words and a joke for each.

"I should have said goodbye to Madame also, but . . ."

"Madame is in, I'll . . ."

Emma was gone for a moment; then she was back again.

"Madame has a headache and has gone to lie down on the sofa. But she sends her best wishes."

"Come again!" said all the girls as I left.

I tucked my sack under my arm and set out on my way. Suddenly I remembered the ax: Falkenberg might be looking for it and not finding it. So I went back, knocked on the kitchen window, and left a message about the ax.

As I walked down the road, I turned around once or twice and looked back toward the windows of the house. Finally the whole place disappeared from view.

XXVI

I circled round Øvrebø all day long, in and out of farms in search of work, a roving, aimless outcast. The weather was cold and raw; only my restless wandering kept me warm.

Toward evening I made for my former place of work among the Captain's timber. No ax blows reached my ears; Falkenberg had gone home. I found the trees I had felled in the night and roared with laughter at the appalling stumps I had left. Falkenberg must have seen the wanton destruction and speculated on who its perpetrator might be. Perhaps the good Falkenberg had concluded it was a ghost, and this was why he had fled back home while the daylight lasted. Ha-ha-ha!

My merriment was not, of course, the healthy kind, being the result of my fever in the night and subsequent faintness; and very soon I was feeling sad again. Here on this very spot she had stood one day with her friend; they had come out to us in the forest and had chatted with us . . .

When it was well and truly dark, I set off for the manor. Perhaps I could spend one more night in the loft, and tomorrow when her headache was gone, she would come out. I came near enough to see the lights of the farm and then turned back. Perhaps it was still too early.

For two hours, I reckon, I wandered and sat, wandered and sat; then I approached the manor again. I could perfectly well go up in the loft and sleep there—let the miserable Falkenberg grumble if he dare! Ah, now I knew what to do: I would hide my sack in the forest before showing up, so as to look as if I had merely come back for some small item I had forgotten.

I went back to the forest.

Only when I had hidden the sack did I realize that Falkenberg and the loft and the bed there were no concern of mine. I was an ass and a simpleton: for me it was not a question of finding a place for the night but of seeing one particular person and then putting the manor and the entire parish behind me. My dear sir, I said to myself, weren't you the one who was going to seek out the quiet life and healthy people, and regain your peace of mind?

I drew the sack from its hiding place again, slung it on my back, and for the third time advanced on the manor. I skirted the servants' hall and reached the south side of the main building. There was a light in the living room.

And now, although it was dark, I lowered the sack from my shoulder so as not to be taken for a beggar, tucked it under my arm like a parcel, and cautiously approached the house. When I had come near enough I stopped. I stood, erect and strong, in front of the living-room windows, took off my cap, and remained standing there. There was no one to be seen indoors, not even a shadow. The dining room was dark, the evening meal was over. It must be quite late in the evening, I told myself.

Suddenly the lamp in the living room went out, and the whole house looked deserted. I waited for a while; then a solitary light appeared in an upstairs room. It was *her* room! Or so I thought. The light burned for half an hour or so and then went out. Now she had gone to bed. Good night.

Good night forever.

For of course I had no intention of returning here in the spring. Not on your life.

On coming down to the main road, I heaved the sack up on my shoulder again and set out on my wanderings . . .

Next morning I continued on my way. I had lain in a barn, frozen stiff for want of bedclothes; moreover, I had had to leave at the coldest hour of dawn, to avoid being discovered.

I walked and walked. The forest was sometimes evergreens and sometimes birch. Seeing a cluster of fine, straight-stemmed junipers, I cut myself a staff from one and sat by the edge of the forest whittling it down. A few yellow leaves still clung to the trees; but the birches were one mass of male catkins hung with pearls of rain. From time to time half a dozen small birds would swoop down on one of these birches and peck at the catkins, then look for a stone or a rough tree trunk and rub the gum from off their beaks. No give-and-take among these birds: there were a million catkins to plunder, but still they pursued each other and chased each other away. And the one pursued had no recourse but to flee. If a small bird bore down on a larger bird, the latter was forced away; even a large thrush never thought of resisting a sparrow, but merely swerved to one side. I supposed it must have been the attacker's speed that made him dangerous.

Gradually my early-morning shivers and malaise wore off, and I amused myself observing the various things I met with on my way and thinking random thoughts about each one. The birds entertained me most. It exhilarated me, also, to think that my pockets were full of money.

The previous morning Falkenberg had chanced to mention where Peter's home was; and now I headed in that direction. It was a small farm, where I was unlikely to find work; but now that I was rich, work no longer had pride of place in my thoughts. Peter should be coming home very soon and might have something to tell me.

I arranged things so as to reach Peter's home in the evening. I brought tidings from the son of the house: he was very much better and would soon be coming home. And could they give me a roof for the night?

XXVII

I had been there a couple of days; Peter had come home, but could tell me nothing.

"Everything all right at Øvrebø?"

"I heard nothing to the contrary."

"Did you see them all before you left? The Captain, Madame?"

"Yes."

"Nobody sick?"

"No. Who did you have in mind?"

"Falkenberg," I said. "He was complaining about an injury to his hand; seems like it must be all right again."

It was a cheerless home, though prosperous enough. The master of the house was a deputy member of the Storting, and had taken to sitting and reading the newspapers of an evening. The whole household wilted under this infernal reading, and the daughters were bored to death. When Peter arrived home, the entire family set to work calculating whether he had been paid in full and whether he had been lying sick at the Captain's expense for the full permitted period—the full *statutory* period, said the politician. And when I was unlucky enough to break a paltry little windowpane, there were whisperings and black looks in my direction from every quarter. The next day I went to the local store, bought a new pane, and fixed it in neatly with putty—whereupon the politician said, "You really shouldn't have gone to all that trouble for the sake of a windowpane."

But it wasn't only for the sake of the windowpane that I went to the store: I bought in addition two or three bottles of wine, to show I wasn't fussed over the price of a windowpane or two, and likewise a sewing machine, as a present for the girls when I left. We could drink the wine that evening, since tomorrow was Sunday, when we would all have time to sleep late. But on Monday morning I meant to resume my wanderings.

In the event, things turned out rather differently. The two girls had been up in the loft, poking around in my sack; both the sewing machine and the bottles had put ideas in their heads; they formed their conclusions about these objects and began dropping hints. Take it easy, girls, all in my own good time!

That evening I was sitting in the living room chatting with the family. We had just had supper, and the master of the house had put on his spectacles and addressed himself to the newspapers. From outside came the sound of a throat being cleared. "There's someone there," I said. The girls looked at each other and went out. A moment later they threw the door open and ushered in two young men. "Come in and sit down," said the wife.

It dawned on me at once that these two young yokels had been sent for apropos my wine and that they were the two girls' beaux. Such promising fillies—eighteen, nineteen, and already as clever as they come! But wine was simply not on the menu, no, not one drop . . .

The talk was about the weather, how it was no good looking for better weather at this time of year; still, it was bad luck they couldn't go on with the plowing because of the wet. The chit-chat had no life in it, and one of the girls turned to me and asked why I was so quiet.

"I dare say it's because I'm leaving," I replied. "By Monday morning I shall be a dozen miles from here."

"So perhaps we should have a farewell drink tonight?"

There was tittering at this suggestion, as a shrewd thrust at myself, sitting there and hoarding my wine like a miser. But I neither knew nor cared for these girls, or it would have been another story.

"What farewell drink?" I asked. "I've bought three bottles of wine to take where I'm going, that's all."

"Are you really carrying the wine twelve miles?" asked one girl amid loud laughter. "There are plenty of stores on the way, surely?"

"The young lady is forgetting that tomorrow is Sunday," I answered, "when all shops and stores are closed."

The laughter died away, but they liked me no better for telling them where they got off. I turned to the lady of the house and asked resentfully how much I owed.

No hurry, was there? Wouldn't tomorrow be time enough?

Yes, there was a hurry. I had been there two days; better consider the price.

She thought for a long time; finally she left the room, with her husband in tow, for the necessary deliberations.

They were away so long that I went up to the loft, got my sack ready, and carried it down to the entrance. I decided to be even more resentful and to leave that very evening. It would be a good way of making my escape.

When I re-entered the living room, Peter said, "You're not proposing to walk out into the night, are you?"

"That's exactly what I'm proposing to do."

"You shouldn't be so stupid as to care what these wenches say."

"For heaven's sake, let the old man go!" said his sister.

At last the politician and his wife returned. They maintained a stubborn, cautious silence.

Well, how much did I owe?

Hm. It was for me to decide.

The whole brood was trash, and here was I suffocating in the midst of it all. I flung her the first bank note that came to hand.

Was that enough?

Hm. It certainly went some way toward, but. And then again it might be enough, but.

How much was it I had given her?

A five.

Well, perhaps that was a bit on the skimpy side. I felt for more money.

"No, Mother, it was a *ten,*" said Peter. "And that's far too much—you must give him some change."

The old girl opened her fist, looked at the note, and was instantly all astonishment. "Well goodness, gracious me, if it isn't a ten! I didn't look at it properly. In that case, thank you very much."

In his extremity the politician began telling the two boys about what he'd been reading in the newspaper: a nasty accident, hand crushed in a threshing machine. The girls carried on as if they never saw me, though truth to tell they sat like two cats with necks contracted and knife-narrow eyes. Nothing to wait for here—goodbye to the place.

The wife followed me out to the entrance and tried to butter me up. "Be a dear and lend us a bottle of wine. It's so embarrassing with the two boys sitting there."

"Good—bye!" was all I would say: I was not to be spoken to.

I had my sack over my shoulder and the sewing machine in one hand; it weighed a ton and the road had turned to mud, but my heart was light as I walked. It was a tiresome business I had got mixed up in, and I might as well admit that I had shown up as somewhat stingy. Stingy? Not at all. I formed myself into a small committee and pointed out that those confounded girls had tried to entertain their beaux with *my* wine. But wasn't my resentment at bottom merely a symptom of male blood? If the guests had been two strange girls instead of the two boys, would the wine not then have flowed? Surely! And "the old man," she had said. But was she not right? I must indeed have become old to make such an issue of being pushed aside in favor of a plowboy . . .

But as I trudged along my resentment wore off, the committee was dissolved, and I walked for hour after hour with my ridiculous burden: three bottles of wine and a sewing machine.

The weather was mild and misty, so that I saw farmhouse lights only when I was already quite near; then, usually, the dogs would rush out at me and prevent me from sneaking into a barn. The hour grew later and later; I was weary and woebegone and beset with anxieties about the future. Why, oh why, had I squandered so much of my money, and all to no purpose? I had better sell the sewing machine and convert it back into cash.

At long last I came to a cottage with no dog. There was still a light in the window, and without more ado I went in and asked for shelter.

XXVIII

The only person in the living room was a girl of fifteen or so who sat at a table sewing. When I asked for shelter she replied, in the most trustful possible way, that she would ask; then she disappeared into a small adjoining room. I called after her that I could manage very nicely just sitting here by the stove until the morning.

After a short interval the girl came back with her mother, who was still fastening and buttoning her clothes. Good evening! Well, they hadn't the space to make me really comfortable, but I was welcome to sleep in the other little room.

Where would they sleep themselves, then?

Oh, it would soon be morning now. Besides, the girl was going to sit up and sew for quite a while yet.

What was she sewing? A dress?

No, only a dressy skirt. She was to wear it for church tomorrow, but hadn't wanted to let her mother help her.

I produced my sewing machine and said jokingly that one dressy skirt more or less meant nothing to a fellow like this! Just let me show her!

Was I a tailor by any chance?

No. But I sold sewing machines.

I picked up the directions and read aloud what we had to do, while the girl listened attentively; she was only a child, with slender fingers all blue from the dye coming off. These blue fingers were so pitiful to see that I brought out the wine and poured some for each of us. Then we continued sewing, I with the directions in my hand, the girl turning away on the machine. "It's going splendidly," she said, and her eyes glowed.

How old was she?

Sixteen. Confirmed last year.

What was her name?

Olga.

Her mother stood watching us and wanting to have a go on the machine; but every time she came near it, Olga said, "Careful, Mother, you mustn't mantreat it!" And when the spool needed filling and her mother got hold of the shuttle for a moment, Olga was again afraid of its being mantreated.

The mother put on the coffeepot and made up the fire, the room grew nice and warm; these lonely people were at ease and full of trust, and Olga laughed whenever I thought up a joke about the machine. Although it was for sale, I noticed that neither of them asked how much it cost; it lay far, far beyond their reach. But what a joy to see it in operation!

She should have had a machine like that, should Olga; she had an excellent way with it.

Her mother replied that Olga would have to wait until she had been in service for a while.

Was Olga going into service?

Yes, she hoped so. Both her other daughters were in service—never gave a spot of bother, praise God. Olga was to meet them at church tomorrow.

On one wall hung a little cracked mirror, on the other some cheap prints of soldiers on horseback and royal couples in full regalia. One of the pictures was old and tattered, and showed the Empress Eugénie; hardly a recent purchase. I asked where it had come from.

Couldn't rightly remember. Husband must have picked it up one time or another.

In these parts?

Had an idea it might have been at Hersæt—husband had been in service there in his younger days. Could be thirty years ago.

I had a little plan in my head. I said, "That picture's worth a lot of money."

The woman thought I was making fun of her; so I examined it closely and declared unwaveringly that this was no cheap picture—most certainly not.

The woman was no fool, and only said, Really, did I think so? It had hung there ever since the cottage was built. Anyway, it was Olga's picture; she had regarded it as hers from the time she was little.

I put on a mysterious, knowing manner and asked, as if to get to the bottom of the matter, "And where's Hersæt?"

Hersæt was in the next parish, about twelve miles away. The Sheriff lived there . . .

The coffee was ready, and Olga and I stopped for a break. Only the hooks remained to be put in. I asked if I might see the blouse that went with the skirt; but it seemed there was no real blouse, only a knitted kerchief. But one of her sisters had given her a cast-off jacket, and this jacket was to go outside everything and hide everything.

"Olga's growing so fast at present, it would be madness to think of buying her a proper blouse for a year to come," I was informed.

Olga sat putting in the hooks; and soon the job was done. By now she could hardly keep her eyes open, so I assumed an air of authority and ordered her to bed. Her mother felt obliged to sit up and keep me company, even though I begged her, too, to go back to bed.

"But now," she said to her daughter, "you must thank the kind gentleman properly for all his help."

Whereupon Olga came and took my hand and curtseyed. I saw my chance and shooed her off into the little bedroom.

"And now you'd better go too," I said to her mother. "I won't talk any more now, in any case, because I'm tired."

When she saw me pitching camp by the stove and arranging my sack as a pillow, she laughed, shook her head, and left me to my devices.

XXIX

I am happy and comfortable here; it is morning, the sun shines in through the window, and both Olga and her mother are a joy to behold, with their hair all wet and smoothed.

They shared their breakfast with me, and we drank large quantities of coffee; after which Olga dressed herself up in her new skirt, her knitted kerchief, and her jacket. That marvelous jacket! It had lasting all around the edges, and two rows of buttons of the same material, while the neck and sleeves were trimmed with braid; and it was far, far too big for little Olga, who was thin and bony as a young calf.

"Shall we shorten the jacket a little?" I suggested. "We've time if we're quick."

But mother and daughter glanced at each other, meaning it was Sunday, when needles and knives are things prohibited. I knew well what they were thinking—in my childhood I used to think like that myself—and I tried to save the situation with a little freethinking: ah, but the sewing would be done by a machine and that was different—no worse than when an innocent carriage rolls along the highway on a Sunday.

But no: this they could not follow. Besides, the jacket was meant for growing into; in a year or two it would fit nicely.

I tried to think of something I could slip into Olga's hand as she left, but I had nothing; so I gave her a krone instead. She shook hands and curtseyed again; then she showed the coin to her mother and whispered, her eyes sparkling, that she would give it to her sister at church. And her mother, almost equally moved, agreed that perhaps she should.

So Olga went to church in her overlong jacket, shambling down the slope with her feet turned in and out as chance might take them. Dear God, how sweet and amusing she was . . .

Was Hersæt a big manor?

A big manor, yes.

I sat for a while, blinking my sleepy eyes and playing the etymologist. Hersæt could mean *herresæte:* gentleman's seat. Or a *herse*—a local chieftain—may have ruled there. And the chieftain's daughter is the haughtiest maiden for many a mile, and the jarl himself comes and asks for her hand. And the year after she bears him a son, who becomes king . . .

In short, I planned to go to Hersæt. It was all the same where I went; so I would go there. I might get work from the Sheriff, I might stumble on something or other; at the very least there would be new faces. And having thus decided on Hersæt, I felt I had an aim and an object.

I was drowsy and stupid from lack of sleep; so I got permission to lie down on the mother's bed. A beautiful blue-cross spider wandered slowly up over the wall, and I lay there following it with my eyes until I fell asleep.

I slept for a couple of hours, then suddenly woke, feeling rested and fit. My hostess was cooking the midday dinner. I packed my sack, paid for my bed and board, and ended by saying I'd like to do a swap with Olga: her picture for my sewing machine.

Sheer disbelief again.

It was all one, I said; if she was satisfied, so was I. The picture had its value; I knew what I was doing.

I took the picture down from the wall, blew the dust from it, and rolled it up carefully; it left a rectangle of lighter color on the timber wall. Then I said goodbye.

The woman followed me out: couldn't I wait until Olga came home, so that she could thank me in person? Oh, if only I would!

But I couldn't spare the time. "Tell her, if there's anything she's uncertain about, to look in the directions."

She stood for a long time following me with her eyes. I swaggered along the road, whistling with satisfaction at what I had done. Now I had only the sack to carry, I was rested, the sun shone, and the road had dried out somewhat. Soon I burst out singing with satisfaction at what I had done.

Nerves . . .

I reached Hersæt the following day. It looked such a big and splendid place that at first I felt like walking straight past; but after talking for a while with one of the farmhands, I decided to present myself to the Sheriff. I had worked for rich people before—the Captain at Øvrebø, for example . . .

The Sheriff was a short, broad-shouldered man, with a long white beard and dark eyebrows. His voice was gruff but his eyes were kindly. Later, I found he was a jovial man who enjoyed the occasional joke and a good hearty laugh. At other times he could be self-important about his wealth and position; and he was something of a climber.

"Afraid I've no work for you here. Where have you come from?"

I mentioned some places along my route.

"You've no money, so you go around begging, eh?"

I was *not* begging, and I *had* money.

"Well, you'd better be on your way. Sorry, but I've no work for you here, the plowing season's over. Can you cut stakes for a fence?"

"Yes."

"I see. Well, I don't have wooden fences any more, I've switched to wire. Can you do masonry work?"

"Yes."

"Pity. I've had bricklayers all autumn, you could have lent a hand."

He stood poking the ground with his stick.

"What made you come to me?"

"Everyone said, If you want work, go to the Sheriff."

"Is that so? Well, yes, I'm constantly having all kinds of people in; this autumn it's been the bricklayers. Can you put up a fence that's proof against hens? Because I've yet to meet a living soul who can, ha-ha! Did you say you'd been with Captain Falkenberg at Øvrebø?"

"Yes."

"What were you doing there?"

"Felling timber."

"Don't know the man—his place is a fair distance from here. Still, I've heard of him. Have you got papers from him?"

I handed him the testimonial.

"Right, come with me," said the Sheriff without more ado.

He led me around the house and into the kitchen.

"Give this man a first-rate meal," he said; "he's come a long way." . . .

I sat in the big, bright kitchen and had my best meal for many a day. I had just finished eating when the Sheriff returned.

"You, there," he began—

I rose at once and stood like a sentry—a small courtesy which he evidently did not despise.

"No, go on eating, finish your meal. Finished already? I thought perhaps . . . Come with me."

The Sheriff led me to the woodshed.

"You could do a stint of chopping down firewood, what do you say to that? I've got a couple of men, but I'm using one of them on official business at present, so you'd better go wood-cutting with the other. I've plenty of firewood, as you can see, but there's room for more—one can never have too much of the stuff. You said you had money; let me see."

I showed him my bank notes.

"Good. You see, I represent the government, which means I have to keep tabs on my own men. Still, it's obvious you've nothing on your conscience or you wouldn't have come to the Sheriff, ha-ha-ha! Well, as I was saying, you can take it easy today and start chopping down firewood tomorrow."

I began busying myself with preparations for the morrow: getting my clothes in order, sharpening the saw and the ax. I had no mittens, but it was not yet the weather for mittens; otherwise I lacked for nothing.

Several times the Sheriff came out and talked of this and that; he enjoyed talking to me, no doubt, stranger and wanderer that I was. "Come here, Margaret!" he called to his wife as she crossed the courtyard. "This is the new man—I'm getting him to chop down firewood."

XXX

We had no detailed instructions, so we used our intelligence and began by felling only dead trees; and in the evening the Sheriff told us we had done right. The remaining timber he would select for us in the morning.

I soon saw that our present work was not going to last until Christmas. With the weather we were having—light frost at night but no snow—and the ground as it was, there was nothing to hold us up, and we felled a mass of timber every day; as the Sheriff himself put it, we were cutting down trees like a pair of maniacs, ha-ha-ha! The old man was easy to work for; he visited us frequently in the forest, always in a good humor, and since I seldom answered in the same joking vein, he doubtless concluded I was a dull dog, though a reliable one. After a while he started sending me to the post office, fetching and carrying official letters.

There were no children about the place, and no young people except for the maids and one of the hands, so the evenings tended to drag. I amused myself by getting hold of some tin and some acids, and tin-plating a number of old kettles in the kitchen. But this didn't last me for long. Then one evening I sat down and wrote the following letter:

> If only I were where you are, I would work hard enough for two!

The next day, when I had to go to the post office for the Sheriff, I took my letter too and posted it. I was in a great state of agitation; the letter even had a slightly uncouth appearance, the result of my borrowing stationery from the Sheriff and having to plaster a whole string of stamps over his name printed on the envelope. What on earth would she say when she got it? The letter was unsigned and gave no return address.

Well, we worked in the woods, the lad and I, exchanged small talk, labored with might and main, and were the best of friends. The days went by, and the end of the work, alas, was already in sight; but I still nursed a faint hope that the Sheriff might find something else for me to do when the woodcutting was finished. Something was sure to turn up. I had no desire to start wandering again before Christmas.

Then one day, while visiting the post office again, I was handed a letter. I could not grasp that it was for me and stood there irresolutely, turning it over and over; but the postmaster, who knew me by now, glanced at the envelope again and confirmed that it was addressed to me, care of the Sheriff. A sudden thought struck me and I clutched the letter. Yet, it was for me, I was forgetting . . . yes, it was true . . .

Bells began ringing in my ears, I hurried out into the road, opened the letter, and read:

Don't *write* to me—

No name, no address, but crystal-clear and lovely. The second word was underlined.

How I got home I don't know. I remember sitting by the side of the road on a guardstone, reading the letter, sticking it in my pocket, and then walking on to another guardstone and repeating the process. Don't *write*. Could I, then, come and maybe talk with her? This exquisite little paper, this flowing, elegant hand! Her fingers had encircled this letter, it had lain before her eyes, it was perfumed with her breath. And then at the end a dash: there could be a world of meaning in that dash.

I came home, delivered the mail, and went into the forest. I was lost in dreams, and doubtless incomprehensible to my companion as he saw me, time and time again, reading a letter and then putting it safely away with my money.

How clever of her to find me! She must have held the envelope up to the light and read the Sheriff's name under the stamps; then tilted her beautiful head on one side for a moment, blinked her eyes, and thought, So now he is working for the Sheriff at Hersæt . . .

When we were back home that evening, the Sheriff came out to us, talked about this and that, then asked, "Wasn't it Captain Falkenberg at Øvrebø you said you'd worked for?"

"Yes."

"I see he's invented a machine."

"A machine?"

"A felling saw. It's in the papers."

I gave a start. Surely he hadn't invented *my* felling saw?

"There must be some mistake," I said; "it wasn't the Captain who invented the saw."

"No?"

"No, indeed. Though the saw was left with him."

I told the Sheriff everything. He went in to get the paper, and we read together: "New invention . . . our special correspondent . . . sawing technique of great potential importance to owners of forest land . . . principle of the mechanism is as follows . . ."

"You're not telling me it's you who invented it?"

"I most certainly am."

"And the Captain's trying to steal it, eh? That will make a jolly little case, an extraordinarily jolly little case. Leave it to me. Did anyone see you working on the invention?"

"Yes, everyone in the place."

"Damned if it isn't the most brazen thing I ever heard! Stealing your invention! Think of the money—it could reach the million mark!"

I had to confess that I couldn't understand the Captain.

"I understand him all right; I'm not Sheriff for nothing. I've had my eye on that man for a long time now—he's not so deucedly rich as he makes out. Now he's going to get a little letter from *me,* quite a short little letter—what do you say to that? Ha-ha-ha! Leave it to me."

But now I became uneasy: the Sheriff was too hasty—the Captain could well be innocent, the reporter could have been inaccurate. I begged the Sheriff to let me write myself.

"And agree to go halves with the scoundrel? Never! You leave the whole thing in my hands. Besides, if you write, you won't do it in style, the way I would."

But I coaxed and coaxed, until finally it was agreed that I should write the first letter and that he should step in at a later stage. I got some more of his writing paper.

There was no writing done that evening; the excitements of the day had left me in a state of inner turmoil. I brooded and reflected; for Madame's sake I would avoid writing direct to the Captain, which might make things awkward for her; instead, I would drop a line to my mate Falkenberg, asking him to keep an eye on the machine.

That night I had another visit from the corpse, from this miserable shrouded woman who gave me no peace over her thumbnail. After the prolonged agitation of the day, she made sure to visit me in the night. Chilled to the bone with terror, I saw her come gliding in, stop in the middle of the floor, and hold out her hand. By the other wall, directly opposite, my workmate lay in his bed, and it was with a strange sense of relief that I heard him groaning and tossing about; that meant there were two of us in danger. I shook my head, meaning that I had buried the nail in a peaceful spot and could do no more. But the corpse continued to stand there. I begged her to forgive me; but suddenly I was seized with anger and told her furiously that I would put up with her nonsense no longer. I had only borrowed her nail in an emergency, and it was months since I had done what I could and buried it again . . . At this she came gliding sideways over to my pillow and tried to get behind me. I flung myself forward and up, and let out a shriek.

"What is it?" asked the lad in the other bed.

I rubbed my eyes and said it was only a dream.

"Who was that in here?" asked the boy.

"I don't know. Was anyone in here?"

"I saw someone go . . ."

XXXI

I let two days go by; then I sat down calmly and loftily to write to Falkenberg. I had left a little sawing device behind at Øvrebø, I wrote; it might one day acquire a certain importance for owners of forest land, and I intended to come and collect it in the near future. Please keep an eye on it and see that nothing happens to it.

Such a mild letter—the most dignified line to take. In case Falkenberg should mention it in the kitchen, as well he might, and perhaps even show it around, it must be the soul of delicacy. But it was not just mildness and more mildness and nothing but mildness, for, to show I was in earnest, I added a definite date: I would collect the machine on Monday the eleventh of December.

I thought: This deadline makes it clear and explicit: if on that Monday the machine is not there, then something is going to be done about it.

I posted the letter myself, and again plastered the envelope with a string of stamps . . .

I was still in a state of delicious ecstasy: I had received the loveliest letter in the world, I carried it here in my breast pocket, it was to *me*. Don't *write*. No, indeed, but I could come. And the letter ended with a dash.

Surely there was nothing wrong about that underlining—it could not, for example, merely be intended to emphasize the prohibition in a general way? Ladies were terrors for underlining every possible word and sprinkling dashes here, there, and everywhere. But not her, never her!

A few days more and the work at the Sheriff's would be finished; it all fitted nicely, everything worked out, on the eleventh I should be at Øvrebø! And perhaps not a moment too soon: if it was really the case that the Captain had designs on my machine, I needed to move fast. Was a stranger to steal my hard-earned million? Had I not toiled for it? I began almost to regret the mildness of my letter to Falkenberg: it could have been considerably sharper: now he might not believe that I was any kind of tough guy. Who knows, he might even have the nerve to bear witness against me and deny that I'd invented the machine. Ho-ho, my good friend Falkenberg, just you try! If you do, you will forfeit your eternal salvation for a start; and in case that isn't enough, I shall tell on you for perjury, to my friend and patron the Sheriff. And you know what will happen then.

"But of course you must go," said the Sheriff when I talked to him. "And by all means bring the machine back here. You have to look after your own interests—there may be large sums involved."

Next day the post brought an item of news which transformed the situation at a stroke: a letter in the newspaper from Captain Falkenberg himself, saying that the attribution to himself of the construction of a new felling saw rested on a misunderstanding. Credit for the invention was due, on the contrary, to a man who had worked for a time on his estate. About the machine itself he wished to express no opinion. Captain Falkenberg.

The Sheriff and I looked at each other.

"What do you make of that?" he asked.

"That the Captain, at all events, is innocent."

"So. Do you know what I think?"

Pause. The Sheriff a sheriff from top to toe, a man who recognizes an intrigue when he sees one.

"He is *not* innocent," he said.

"Do you really think so?"

"I'm used to this sort of thing. Now he's drawing in his horns; your letter has given him warning. Ha-ha-ha!"

So I had to confess to the Sheriff that, far from addressing myself to the Captain, I had merely dropped a line to one of the hands at Øvrebø, and that not even this letter could have arrived yet, since it had been posted only the evening before.

This struck the Sheriff speechless, and he gave up trying to recognize intrigues. On the other hand, he seemed from this moment to have doubts about the value of the entire invention.

"It may well be that the machine's a dud," he said, adding good-naturedly, "I mean, it may need modifying and improving. You must have noticed how they're constantly having to change the design of warships and flying machines . . . Are you still set on going?"

After this I heard no more about my coming back and bringing the machine with me; but the Sheriff gave me a good testimonial. He would gladly have kept me on longer, it said, but the work was interrupted by my having private interests elsewhere to look after . . .

Next morning, just as I was leaving, I found a young girl standing outside in the courtyard waiting for me. It was Olga. Was there ever such a child? She must have been on her feet since midnight to get here so early. There she stood in her blue skirt and her jacket.

"Hello, Olga! Where are you off to?"

She had come to see me.

How did she know I was here?

She had asked here and there. Was it true, please, that she was to have the sewing machine? Surely it couldn't—

Yes, indeed the machine was hers; I had got her picture in exchange. Was it working well?

Yes, it was working well.

We exchanged only a few words; I wanted to get rid of her before the Sheriff came out and started asking questions.

"And now you must go home, child. You've a long way to go."

Olga gave me her hand; it was completely buried in mine, and lay there as long as I chose to keep it. Then she thanked me and shambled cheerfully away, her toes turned in and out as chance might take them.

XXXII

I had nearly reached my goal.

That Sunday night I slept at a little cottage near Øvrebø in order to arrive at the manor early on Monday morning. By nine they would all be up—when, surely, I must be lucky enough to meet the one I sought!

By now I was a bundle of nerves and kept picturing to myself all manner of evils: my letter to Falkenberg had been perfectly proper and free from abuse, but the Captain might, nevertheless, have taken umbrage over that accursed date, that deadline I had set him. Would to God I had never sent any letter!

As I approached the place, I stooped more and more and shrank into myself, even though I had committed no offense. I left the road and made a detour so as to reach the outbuildings first—and there I met Falkenberg. He stood washing down the carriage. We greeted each other and were the same good friends as before.

Was he taking the carriage out somewhere?

No, he had only just got back last night. Been to the station to catch a train.

Who was catching the train?

Madame.

Madame?

Madame.

Pause.

Well, well. Where was Madame going?

Spending a few days in town.

Pause.

"A stranger's been here and written about your machine in the papers," said Falkenberg.

"Has the Captain gone too?"

"No, the Captain's at home. He really looked down his nose when your letter came."

I lured Falkenberg up to our old loft. My sack still contained two bottles of wine, which I now brought out and opened. Aha! These bottles, which I had carried to and fro for mile after mile, and which had needed such careful handling, were now proving their worth. But for them Falkenberg would not have said nearly so much.

"Why did the Captain look down his nose about my letter? Did he see it?"

"It all started," said Falkenberg, "with Madame being in the kitchen when I brought the post. 'What's that letter with all those stamps on?' she asked. I opened it and said it was from you and you'd be here on the eleventh."

"What did she say to that?"

"She didn't say anything. Just asked again, 'Coming on the eleventh, is he?' 'That's right,' I said."

"And two days later you were told to drive her to the station?"

"Yes, it must have been about two days later. So then I said to myself: Since Madame knows about the letter, I suppose the Captain ought to know about it too. Do you know what he said when I showed it to him?"

I didn't answer; I was thinking and thinking. Was there something behind all this? Was she running away from me? I must be mad—the Captain's wife at Øvrebø doesn't go running away from one of her workmen. But it looked very strange to me. I had hoped to be allowed to talk to her since I was forbidden to write.

Falkenberg continued a shade uneasily, "I showed the Captain your letter, you see, even though you hadn't said I should. Was that wrong of me?"

"Oh, never mind. What did he say, then?"

" 'Well, you'd better take good care of the machine, hadn't you?' he said, pulling a bit of a face. 'So that nobody comes and takes it,' he said."

"Is the Captain angry with me now, then?"

"Oh no. No, I can't believe that. And I've heard no more about it since."

Never mind about the Captain. When Falkenberg had drunk a fair quantity of wine, I asked him if he knew Madame's address in town. No, but Emma might. We got hold of Emma, gave her some wine, talked of this and that, circled around the question, getting nearer and nearer, and finally asked it in the discreetest possible way. No, Emma didn't know the address.

But Madame was doing her Christmas shopping and had traveled with Miss Elizabeth from the parsonage, so the people there would probably know the address. What did I want it for, in any case?

I had picked up an old filigree brooch and thought I might ask if she'd care to buy it from me.

"Let's have a look."

Fortunately I was able to show Emma the brooch, a beautiful old piece of work which I had bought from one of the maids at Hersæt.

"Madame won't want that," said Emma. "And no more would I."

"Oh yes, you would, Emma, if you got me in the bargain," I said with forced jocularity.

Exit Emma. I pumped Falkenberg again. Falkenberg had a good nose for such things, there were times when he understood people.

Did he still sing for Madame?

No, he did not. And Falkenberg was sorry he had signed on; there seemed to be more and more weeping and sorrow about the place.

Weeping and sorrow? Were the Captain and Madame not on good terms, then?

Lord, yes, they were on good terms—as they'd always been. Last Saturday she was in tears all day.

"I can't make that out—they're always so civil and straight with each other," I said, and waited for his reply.

"Yes, and so bored," said Falkenberg. "She's lost a lot of weight too, even in the time since you left—gone terribly thin and pale."

I sat for a couple of hours in the loft, keeping an eye on the main building from my window, but the Captain never showed up. Why did he stay indoors? It was hopeless waiting any longer; I would have to go, without making my excuses to the Captain. There were plenty of good excuses I could have made: I could have blamed the newspaper article, with some justification, for making me mildly megalomaniac. Now it only remained to bundle the machine together, cover it up with my sack as best I could, and set out on my wanderings again.

Emma went into the kitchen and stole some food for me before I left.

I had another long trek ahead of me: first to the parsonage—which, as it happened, lay almost directly on my path—and then to the railroad station. A little light snow was falling, which made the going none too easy; moreover, instead of dawdling as I would have liked, I was obliged to make a forced march: the ladies were only going to town for their Christmas shopping, and they had a head start already.

On the following afternoon I arrived at the parsonage. I had worked out that my best chance was to get talking with the priest's wife.

"I'm on my way into town," I told her. "And here I am, carrying a machine around with me—may I leave the heaviest of the woodwork here?"

"Going into town, are you?" she asked. "But surely you'll stay here for tonight?"

"No, thank you kindly. I have to be in town by tomorrow."

She pondered awhile and said, "Elizabeth's in town. You could take her a parcel, something she's forgotten."

I thought: Aha, the address!

"But there's something I'd need to get ready first."

"In that case, mightn't Miss Elizabeth have left before I arrive?"

"No, no, she's with Mrs. Falkenberg, they're staying there a week."

This was a pleasant piece of news, a glorious piece of news. Now I had both the address and the length of stay.

Madame stood there, gave me a sidelong glance, and said, "You'll stay for the night, won't you? Because there really is something I need to put in order . . ."

I was given a room in the house, since it was now too cold for the hayloft. And when the household had settled down for the night and everything was quiet, Madame came to my room with the parcel and said, "Excuse my coming at this hour. But you may want to leave first thing in the morning, before I'm up."

XXXIII

So here I was, back in the city, with its noise and bustle and newspapers and people; finding, after all these months, that I had nothing really against it. I spent a morning collecting my scattered wits, picked up some different clothes, and set off to call on Miss Elizabeth. She was staying with relatives.

Would I be lucky enough this time to meet the other? I was as nervous as a kitten, and so boorishly unused to gloves that I pulled them off; but as I climbed the steps I saw that my hands did not match my clothes and pulled the gloves on again. Then I rang the bell.

"Miss Elizabeth? Yes, if you wouldn't mind waiting a moment."

Miss Elizabeth came out. "Good afternoon. Was it me you wanted . . . ? Why, it's *you!*"

I had a parcel for her from her mother. Here.

She ripped the parcel open and peered inside. "No! Mother really is unique! The opera glasses. We've been to the theater already . . . I didn't recognize you at first."

"Really? And yet it's not all that long."

"No, only . . . Tell me, isn't there someone else you'd like to ask about? Ha-ha-ha!"

"Yes."

"She's not here. It's only me staying here, with some of my family. She's at the Victoria."

"Well, it was you I brought the parcel for," I said, trying to master my disappointment.

"Wait a bit, I'm just going out again, we can go together."

Miss Elizabeth wrapped herself up, stuck her head in at a door, called out, "Goodbye for now," and followed me out. We took a cab and drove to a quiet café. Miss Elizabeth thought it was *such* fun going to cafés. But this one was no fun at all.

Would she rather go somewhere else?

Yes. To the Grand.

I feared I would be unsafe there; I had been away so long that I might be dragged into saying hello to my acquaintances. But Mademoiselle insisted on the Grand. After only a few days' practice she was already full of self-confidence. But I had been so fond of her before.

We drove off again to the Grand. It was getting on toward evening. Mademoiselle sat herself down where the lights were most dazzling; radiant, herself, over what fun it all was. I ordered wine.

She laughed and said, "Why, how smart you've become!"

"I could hardly come in here in my smock."

"No, of course not. Though, to be honest, that smock . . . Shall I tell you what I think?"

"Please do."

"The smock suited you better."

There now, devil take these town clothes! I sat there, my head afire with other things, and snapped my fingers at this chatter.

"Are you staying in town for long?" I asked.

"It's up to Louise; we've done what we came to do. Oh dear, it's much too short . . ." Then she cheered up again and asked with a laugh, "Did you enjoy being with us in the country?"

"Yes, it was a good time, that."

"Are you coming again soon? Ha-ha-ha!"

It seemed to me she was just sitting there making fun of me: showing that she saw through me, that I hadn't properly learned my lines for my rustic role. The chit! I who could teach a workman his job and was master of several trades! Although in my true calling only my second-best dreams came true.

"Shall I ask Papa to put up a notice in the spring, saying you undertake all kinds of plumbing work?"

She closed her eyes and laughed her ringing laugh.

I was tense, agitated, and pained by this jocularity, however kindly intentioned. I looked around the café to collect myself, saw hats raised here and there, and raised my own, but felt miles away from it all. It was my attractive young companion who drew people's attention.

"You know these people, then?"

"Oh, one or two . . . Have you had a good time in town?"

"Fabulous. I've got two cousins, both boys, and they have various friends."

"Poor young Eric, back home!" I said as a joke.

"You and your young Eric. No, here it's somebody called Bewer. Only I've just fallen out with him."

"That will soon pass."

"Do you think so? Anyway, it's quite serious. Do you know, I'm half expecting him to come here now."

"If he does, you must point him out to me."

"I thought, as we were driving here, you and I could sit here and make him jealous."

"Good, let's do that."

"Yes, but. Well, you ought really to be a bit younger for that. I mean—"

I forced a laugh. "Oh, we'll manage all right. Don't despise us old fogeys, us Methuselahs, we're a match for anyone at times. Just let me sit with you on the banquette, so he doesn't see my bald patch."

Ah, how hard it is to manage the fateful transition to old age gracefully and calmly! Instead, convulsions, writhings, grimaces, strife with the younger generation, envy.

"Please, Miss Elizabeth," I began, and implored her with all my heart, "couldn't you go to the telephone and get Mrs. Falkenberg to come here now?"

She considered the request.

"Yes, let's do that," she said, taking pity on me.

We went to the telephone, rang the Victoria, and were connected with Madame.

"Is that you, Louise? You'll never guess who I'm with—can you come and join us? That's good. We're at the Grand. No, I won't tell you. Yes, of course, it's a man, only he's a gentleman now—I won't say more. Are you coming, then? What's that, you're having second thoughts? Family? Yes yes, you must do as you please, only—yes, he's right beside me now. You *are* in a hurry, aren't you? Well, goodbye then."

Miss Elizabeth rang off and said tersely, "Going to a family gathering."

We went back to our places and had some more wine; I tried to strike a festive note and suggested champagne. Yes, please.

As we sat there, Mademoiselle said, "There's Bewer. Our drinking champagne now couldn't be better."

Engrossed as I was with one subject, and asked now to show my paces and captivate the young lady to another's advantage, I started saying one thing and meaning another—a ploy certain to misfire. I was incapable of getting that telephone conversation out of my head: she must have smelled a rat, guessed it was me waiting for her. But what crime had I committed? Why on earth had I been discharged so abruptly from Øvrebø and Falkenberg taken on in my place? Maybe the Captain and Madame were not always the best of friends, but the husband had scented danger in my presence there and wanted to save his wife from quite so ludicrous a fall. And so now she went around feeling ashamed that I had worked at her place, that she had used me as her coachman and shared two picnic lunches with me. Ashamed, too, of my advancing years . . .

"This won't do at all," said Miss Elizabeth.

So I exerted myself again and said so many crazy things that she started laughing. I drank liberally and grew bolder in my flights of fancy, until finally she seemed to imagine I was genuinely making up to her, with no one else in mind. She began eyeing me.

"Really and truly, you find me rather attractive?"

"Now listen, please—it's Mrs. Falkenberg I'm talking about."

"Sh!" she said. "Of course, it's Mrs. Falkenberg, I've known that all along, only you don't need to say so. I do believe it's beginning to have some effect on that fellow over there. Keep it up, don't let's lose interest."

So she had never imagined I was making up to her with no one else in mind. I was too old for that sort of thing, damn and blast it all.

"But you can't have Mrs. Falkenberg, you know," she began again. "It's hopeless."

"No, I can't have her, and I can't have you either."

"Are you talking to Mrs. Falkenberg again?"

"No, I'm talking to you now."

Pause.

"Did you know I was in love with you once? Yes, I was, back at home."

"This is getting amusing," I said, shifting up on the banquette. "Yes, now we're really going to give it to Bewer."

"Fancy, I used to go up to the churchyard in the evenings just to meet you. But you were too stupid to understand a thing."

"I take it you're talking to Bewer now," I said.

"No, it's the honest truth I'm telling you. And once I came

over to see you in the potato field. It wasn't your young Eric I came to see."

"Fancy its being me!" I said, and made a great show of melancholy.

"Yes, I'm sure you find it strange. But don't forget, we country folks too need someone to get fond of."

"Does Mrs. Falkenberg say that too?"

"Mrs. Falkenberg—no, she says she never wants to get fond of anyone, she only wants to play the piano and that sort of thing. But I was speaking for myself. Do you know what I did once? No, I'm darned if I'll tell you. Do you want to hear?"

"I'm dying to hear."

"Yes, because after all I'm just a little girl in relation to you, so it doesn't matter: it was when you were sleeping in the hayloft at home; I crept up there once and straightened your blankets and made them into a proper bed."

"So it was you who did that!" I exclaimed spontaneously; I was forgetting my lines.

"You ought to have seen me creeping in, ha-ha-ha!"

But the girl was not yet practiced enough: she changed color over her little confession and tried to cover up with a forced laugh.

To help her out I said, "All the same now, you're a splendid creature. Mrs. Falkenberg could never had done a thing like that."

"No, but then she's older. Or did you think we were the same age?"

"And Mrs. Falkenberg says she never wants to get fond of anyone?"

"Yes. Oof, no really, I don't know. Mrs. Falkenberg's married, you see, she doesn't say anything. Now, talk to me a bit again . . . Yes, and then there was the time we were to go to the store together, do you remember? I kept walking slower and slower so that you would catch up with me . . ."

"That was nice of you. And now I want to make you happy in return."

I got up, went over to young Bewer, and asked him if he would care to have a glass with us, at our table. I fetched him along, while Miss Elizabeth turned red as a beet root. Next I chatted the two youngsters well and truly together; after which I remembered that I had some business to see to and would have to leave them—very reluctantly, ladies and gentlemen. "You indeed, Miss Elizabeth, have completely bewitched me; but I can see I stand no chance. And in any case, it's a mystery now to me . . ."

XXXIV

I drifted along to the town hall square and stood for a while among the cab drivers, watching the entrance to the Victoria. But it was true, of course: she was at a family gathering that evening. So I wandered into the hotel and spoke to the porter.

"Yes, the lady is in. Room number 12, second floor."

"She hasn't gone out, then?"

"No."

"Is she leaving soon?"

"She hasn't said anything."

I came out again, and the cab drivers all sat up and called out, "Cab, sir?" I chose a cab and got in.

"Where to?"

"We'll stay here. I'll pay you by the hour."

The cab drivers began forming little groups and whispering their various opinions: he's watching the hotel, bet you it's his wife in there with a traveling salesman.

Yes, I was watching the hotel. There were scattered lights in the rooms, and it suddenly struck me that she might be up there and see me from a window. "Wait a bit," I said to the cab driver, and went back into the hotel.

"Which floor is number 12?"

"Second floor."

"And does it face the square?"

"Yes."

"Ah, so it *was* my sister who was waving," I said, lying in order to get past the porter.

I went up the stairs, and to give myself no time for second thoughts, I knocked on the door the moment I found the number. No answer. I knocked again.

"Is that the chambermaid?" came from inside.

I could hardly say yes; my voice would have given me away. I tried the door; it was locked. She must have feared my coming; she might even have seen me outside.

"No, it's not the chambermaid," I said, and heard how strangely my words vibrated.

After that I waited for a long time, listening; I could hear someone rustling about inside, but the door remained locked. Then there came two short, sharp rings down to the hall from one of the rooms. It's her, I thought to myself, she's uneasy and has rung for the maid. I moved away from the door so as not to make things awkward for her, and when the maid appeared, I walked past her as if on my way down. I heard the maid say, "Yes, it's the chambermaid." And then the door being opened.

"No, madame," the maid said next, "it was only a gentleman on his way down."

I thought of taking a room in the hotel, but the idea repelled me: she wasn't a married woman on an assignation with a traveling salesman. When I arrived downstairs I simply said to the porter as I passed that the lady seemed to be resting.

Then I went out and sat in the cab again. The time passed, the hour was up, the driver asked if I wasn't cold. Well, yes, a little. Was I waiting for someone? Yes . . . He gave me his blanket from the box, and to reward his kindness I handed him the price of a highball.

The time passed. Hour after hour passed. The cab drivers lost their inhibitions and started saying to each other that I was letting the horses freeze to death.

Oh, what was the use? I paid the driver, went home, and wrote the following letter:

> Since I mustn't *write* to you, may I simply see you again? I will ask for you at the hotel tomorrow afternoon at five o'clock.

Should I make it an earlier hour? But the light in the earlier part of the day was so white, and if I became agitated and my mouth started twitching, I would look ghastly.

I delivered the letter to the Victoria myself and went home again.

A long, long night made up of long, long hours. Just when I needed to sleep and wake up strong and fresh again, I was unable to do so. At dawn I got up, roamed the streets for a long time, drifted back home, lay down, and slept.

The hours passed. On waking and coming to my senses, I hurried straight to the telephone in my anxiety and asked if the lady had left.

No, she had not left.

Thank God, so she didn't mean to run away from me—for she must have had my letter hours ago. No, I had merely chosen an unlucky moment last night, that was all.

I ate some food, lay down, and fell asleep again. When I woke it was long past midday. I stumbled to the telephone again and rang.

No, the lady had not left. But she was packed. She was out at the moment.

I got ready immediately, rushed straight down to the town hall square, and began keeping watch. In the course of half an hour a great many people passed through the hotel doors, but none of them was her. Five o'clock came, and I went in to the porter.

The lady had left.

Left?

"Was it you who telephoned? She came that very moment and took her luggage. But she gave me a letter."

I took the letter and, without opening it, asked about the train.

"The train left at four-forty-five," said the porter, looking at his watch. "It's five o'clock now."

I had squandered half an hour keeping watch outside.

I sat down on one of the steps and stared at my feet. The porter went on talking. He must have known full well that the lady was not my sister.

"I said to the lady that there had just been a gentleman on the telephone. All she said was that she hadn't got time and would I give you this letter."

"Was there another lady with her when she left?"

"No."

I got up and went. Out in the street, I opened the letter and read:

You *must* not follow me about any more—

I stuck it listlessly in my pocket. It held no surprises for me, conveyed no new impressions. Real feminine stuff, words written in haste and on impulse, underlinings and dashes . . .

Then it occurred to me to go to Miss Elizabeth's door and ring; there was still this last faint hope. I heard the bell buzzing inside as I pressed the button and stood listening as if in a whirling wilderness.

Miss Elizabeth had left an hour ago.

So then came more wine, and then came whisky. And then came gallons of whisky. In short, a three-week binge during which a curtain descended on my earthly consciousness. In this condition I had an idea one day: of sending a mirror, with a gay gilt frame, to a certain cottage in the country. It was to go to a little girl by the name of Olga, who was as kind and amusing as a young calf.

Because, you see, I still suffer from nerves.

In my room lies the machine. I can't set it up properly, because most of the woodwork remains in a country parsonage. No matter, my affection for it has grown dim. My fellow neurasthenics, we are poor human beings and not much use, either, as any kind of beast.

One day, I suppose, I shall weary of staying unconscious any longer; then I shall make my way once more to an island.

Born in Norway in 1859, Knut Hamsun is one of the major figures of world literature in the twentieth century, influencing such diverse writers as Henry Miller, Ernest Hemingway, Isaac Bashevis Singer, and Paul Auster.

Hamsun's earliest work included the masterpieces *Hunger*, published in 1890, *Mysteries* (1892) and *Pan* (1894). Among his many other works are *Victoria* (1898), *Under the Autumn Star* (1906), *A Wanderer Plays on Muted Strings* (1909), *Rosa* (1908), *The Last Joy* (1912), *Children of the Age* (1913), *Segelfoss Town* (1915), *The Growth of the Soil* (1917), *The Women at the Pump* (1920), *Chapter the Last* (1923), *Wayfarers* (1927), and *August* (1930). For his writing, Hamsun was awarded the Nobel Prize for Literature.

During World War II, however, Hamsun's reputation was severely damaged when he sided with the Germans as a traitor, events he recounts in his self-analytic and moving autobiography, *On Overgrown Paths*. He died in 1952.

SUN & MOON CLASSICS

Sun & Moon Press's Distinguished List of International Writing